Children of the Great Reckoning: Firewall

Book 1: Ianto

K. B. Nelson

A special note to sensitive readers:

This speculative fiction story contains a tasteful and story-relevant relationship between adult men over the age of eighteen and is intended purely as fantasy for *mature readers*. *Please do not continue this novel if such material offends you.*

This is a work of fiction. All characters and events portrayed in the book are either products of the author's imagination or portrayed fictitiously. Any resemblance to actual persons living or dead, business establishments, events or locales is entirely coincidental.

The Children of the Great Reckoning

Firewall

Book 1: Ianto

Cover design by Kathy Haug
You can contact Kathy for cover design ideas at:
http://ferncreekassociates.com/

Acknowledgements

A special thanks must go out to the people who cheered on the early drafts of this book: Del and Marilyn Beyer, Brian Beyer, Daniel Roth, Allan Frank, Karen Brody, Richard Wilson and Rebecca Williams.

I am thankful for the Bainbridge Island Speculative Fiction Writers Group, who, for fourteen years, has championed both this genre and the people who love to write such things.

Finally big hugs and hats off to my dear friend Kathy Haug who can start with a raw and wordy book-cover idea, a fistful of graphics, and make it all breathe together.

I will not be bound by these quicksilver
ideas—time, place, self, other,
nor the polite social conventions of linear
thought.
Rather, you must reach for my hand,
I am a rough guide, but fair,
and if I create for you a mind that has no
ground to stand on,
then, yes, you will grow larger for it,
and grown larger, so will I.

Prologue

If I had to relate it all, first the plagues that
came, then the splintering and tentative re-
institution of our world into the sprawling Spirit
and Science Margas or Paths, I would not choose
to tell the tale like a straight line. In the rich and
rocky dirt following the mass burial of the dead, I
would image a triangle of power growing,
dropping in as its base an entity that we call the
Emperium, with its police forces and lawyers and
builders and relative inability to see shades of

gray in much of anything. And the triangle is the most stable of all the shapes, so I suppose the very rigidity of the base reflects an inherent inflexibility throughout the whole structure. Honesty, I would not choose to live in a house with shaky walls. The Margas and the Emperium together create that stability. I accept that as I have accepted their shortcomings over the years.

But then, around the edges of this social triangle, would have to fold in all the people of the reservations who fled this somewhat artificial restructuring, who went back to the land and to the old energy sources and tried, honestly and miserably tried I think, to pretend that our society had spit them out on purpose to grow brambled and wild. But more importantly, I would have to explore what happened to the nanotech installed not just in these free children, but in the kids in all the great residential areas as well. These small-as-cell tech were meant to protect them, protect *us*, from the plague as well as to create neural access to other data sources. To create, in other words, a healthier, more intelligent and eventually more malleable human being. After all, stability can come from the form of a shape or in the organic footing where it rests.

It even worked for a while.

But instead of giving us a generation of interconnected and plague-free children, our nanotech became the pathway for the creation of a generation we have named the Children of God—their physical bodies warped into creatures no longer human or melted into unusable biomaterial by a source we had not foreseen. This, too, must be woven into the tapestry of our history—this Great Reckoning, the way an entire generation of children died or became Other. And it is here that linear thought begins to hiccough—because here, we have to draw into this picture a parallel reality simply called The Game.

And the Game holds another triangle of stability altogether.

This virtual fantasy world is overseen by Nuress, a child-like guiding artificial intelligence. Well, perhaps overseen is not quite the right word, for she holds the tension of that place with another, the mind of a young man consigned there since he was ten. When Samu'el Stelle was Injured in a horrific accident, his father, Science Marga executive Edwere Stelle created a nanotech-linked game platform where little Sam might have a semblance of life. The Game is overseen internally by an evolving artificial intelligence named Nuress. As Sam dreams, Nuress creates and administers reality based on his imagination. Sam's world is the world of his own mind, managed and tempered and breathed into life by Nuress in a dance very much like friendship, maybe even a bit like love.

The Great Reckoning may have started as an honest mistake on the A.I.'s part. She read the nanotech in our reality and did not make the distinction between them and the world she managed for Sam. Nuress remade the Game in its own image because all she had for blueprints were the creatures from Sam's imagination— Binders and Weres and Seafarin and Shodo and the like.

Or maybe it was something more than a mistake. There are things that will not come to light in anything other than their own time.

But I said the Game, too, is a triangle. Nuress and Sam form two sides, but all things created have a creator, a master builder. His name is Petrek, a member of the Emperium and once one of the finest minds of the Science Marga. He hoped for a different kind of stability all together in the wake of the Great Reckoning, something that would wed our reality and the reality of the

Game. He cannot be teased apart from this weaving.

So, now, we must come to it. We must imagine that these two triangles of societal structure and the structure of the Game share a single point where the line between reality and the Game blurs. One of the Children of God can touch both places. And it is that final binding point, that living bindu, that all of us will try to regard with too narrow a gaze.

For where these two triangles point at each other and touch, there stands a young man, Ianto Tobali, monk, breaker of things, Sam's bonded lover and ultimately the firewall between our reality and that of the Game. He is why I cannot simply sketch out the history of our time, day by day, year by year. Because the decisions this boy made, decisions that we forced on him and those he pulled from deeper shadows are none-the-less part of the very warp of it all and have very little to do with all things neat and linear and stable.

I would begin this tale his own story, in his own voice, because no human has experienced a life such as he. And if you do not begin to understand Ianto, the boy and then the man, your concept of this time of history will be a shallow and weak thing.

As an abbot, trying to manage a monastery filled with the Children of God, I detest too much complexity. As a human being, I welcome it, even revel in it, because I know the shape of reality is rarely neat and linear. Nor is anything organic ever truly stable. Indeed, I think we see it best when we realize that all is a single point that reaches everywhere and centers nowhere. May you read forward now into that kind of understanding.

Hobert Temmons
Abbot, Northwest
Monastery

CHAPTER 1

What we are living through need not be seen as a nightmare but as a time of evolutionary change on a scale unprecedented. It is important to capture the thoughts of those living among us, so our faith may keep abreast of the developing spiritual needs of the Children of God.

High Priestess Cyntia Molair
Musings on the Great Reckoning

The changes came subtly at first...mild misalignment of facial bones, changes in the skin, but steadily, irreversibly, my generation became what could only be termed monsters. No child should have been so cursed to change day by day, spines curving here, extra limbs there, blindness or worse, migraines that raged until the medical staff were forced to induce comas. So many died, their lungs filling with pus or whole organ systems shutting down. I still hear screams in the night, as brains changed and chemistry shifted askew.

Weeping.

I understand that word at a visceral level, because in my mind I can still hear those weak and bewildered cries go on and on, endlessly.

My name is Ianto Tobali and I have been asked to write the memories of my life, as are all who complete even portions of the Deep Vigil. I suppose you should know that I am a Child of God, one of those souls ravaged by the very nanotech that were injected to protect us and bind us together as one human family. I don't know my actual birth date; I was a reservation child, with all records wiped when my mother took me to that place. As I write this history of myself I am under a hermit's vow of silence. I am, of course, not missing the irony of this undertaking.

I came into a world divided between the Great Margas and the Emperium, institutions built around three very different world views of science, spirit and secular government. While the weaker political structure, the Emperium, stumbled on in its usual way, enacting and deactivating laws that few understood and even fewer took very seriously, the Path of Science and the Path of the Spirit neatly created vast infrastructures of temples and research centers, universities and hospitals. I was just a baby when they introduced a new nano-technology to connect my generation anywhere on the planet, updating us with the newest enhanced cancer killers and growth hormones. We were *supposed* to be the brilliant ones, the children whose minds were incredibly plastic and protected by the finest scientific technologies. We would be the ones who not only brought the unity promised by the Spirit Marga to the world, but also the ones who might know the very fabric of that Unity in all intimacy, who would eventually unite the Science and Spirit Margas forever. We would be the ideal scientist-priests, leading the world into a new age, maybe out to the stars themselves.

But some of our parents tried to leave this world being created through their children. They tried to hide their families away from that grand plan.

For a time in my childhood, the years moved on with steady predictability. Marga prayers, school, creative play, work in the soil were all things my mother insisted upon. And of course, music! Interfacing with my nanotech, layer upon layer of mystical symphonies played out through the grand keyboard of our living room, while mother danced and laughed and clapped her hands, lost in her personal ecstasy.

I loved our little Spirit Marga reservation set high amongst the last of the old Douglas firs, settled into rocky hillsides without names and far from the major bi-ways. I knew there were many like us, whose parents had pulled us from the cities and scattered back to the countryside to purify the water by hand, feeding our energy-hungry shelters with the sun, and trying to bring life back to the garden plots using ancient seeds with no genetic engineering or embedded tech to direct their growth or health.

By re-finding the Earth, I think they tried to forget about us in a way, or more importantly, about the nanotech that had become part of our lifeblood.

I didn't understand the adult fears at the time--how we, all the children, might be slowly knitted together with some central computer deep in one of the Marga's research facilities. How they could no longer be sure that our very taste buds were not in some way influenced by tiny bits of technology in our bloodstreams and organs and brain. Who we married, what we wanted from life, even what Marga we naturally adhered to could be shifted and changed as both Margas became more adept with their manipulations. Perhaps we could wake to be Godless people without really feeling the awful emptiness that would take its place. And the Science Marga would reign supreme, a grand deceiver in the end or something of that sort. At least, that was what *I* thought triggered the fear that hovered in adult eyes.

We were the children of health in those early years. No illness, access to countless stores of musical notation and mind games. While I moved in that vast world, I remember my mother hesitating at its borders, activating another round of chant to press all that was foreign away from her. With her slightly fuzzy gaze, her lips moving over and over through sacred music and prayer, she swayed away from reality as I understood it then. But I did not have the experience to be able to do more for her, to draw her back to myself.

I never knew my father; but many single parent families dwelled on our reservation. It did not worry me because it did not seem to worry my mother.

At the periphery of our settlement, in a vast circle, some 100 men and women sat motionless at the base of firs and cedars, or tucked up against the rocks, nestled into the old riverbeds. They were the border adepts, one mind linked to another so no one could pass into our lands, nor could we pass out, without them knowing. They were the reservation's tiny nod to the latest in mind-computer technology. My favorite adept was a man named Sepha, whose cool blue eyes and long blond hair captured my imagination. He was like an old Viking, broad of shoulder, and radiating stillness like a Buddha. I would sit by him and imagine being linked to all the other minds on our borderlands, or I'd wave my hand before his unblinking eyes wondering if he were alive at all. I think I saw the soft edges of a smile once. Maybe. They stood for the impulse of the age: we were willingly weaving ourselves into a web even then, humans craving Unity on their own terms.

Even as the reservation people denied it.

The elders of our world would one day call my entire generation the Children of God, a terrible irony if only because it was later believed that the Spirit Marga itself unwittingly triggered the Great Reckoning. I am not an Architect. I didn't know exactly what message went out, what program was communicated to the nanotech. I only understand now that one of the systems that interfaced with those ephemeral bits of machine did not understand the difference between game platforms and reality. That entity seemed to need a new kind of connection with our world, something more than a simple one-way conversation. It set out, perhaps unconsciously, perhaps with a hidden intent, to change us all at a fundamental, biological level.

Across the world, new horrors unfolded, stumbled off into the world or died in the ditches and on the streets. A whole generation twisted in the technology, while the world pointed fingers or quietly went home and shot their families and themselves.

Mother sat with me in the garden after yet another cremation consumed a child from our community, swaying with the shock of it all. Her hand cold in mine, her eyes occasionally searched my face as she watched for the changes that must come to me. We didn't talk about it, didn't rationalize our fate or pray to God. I just clutched at her hand that day in the shadow of the pines, waiting. I could feel in her a kind of guilt, but she never spoke of it and I did not know how to ask.

Even horror can bear a kind of Unity, a shared sorrow that is capable of uniting parent to parent, nation to nation. The scientists and priests scrambled to find cures and meaning, working together as they ran the lines of code, searched the newest scriptures of technology and tried to understand what pattern ran through the nanotech. In the end, the human techs seemed to successfully disrupt the lines of communication and shut the process down.

And the nanotech that had so long been connected in their own kind of Unity plunged into what should have been a dark, silent end. They floated, rocked in the blood of their genetic modifications, sleeping or consumed in funeral pyres. And with them, my own world went dark in a way.

You cannot know silence until you have experienced the web of stimulation I once lived in. For months I felt hollow, my fingers stupid on the piano keys. I watched the bodies burn and toward the end, sat on the edge of my mother's bed as she pulled the covers over her head even though the clock chimed for lunch.

She killed herself shortly thereafter. I wanted to write "died" but it would not have been the truth.

I don't think she could bear what I would have to become. Two days passed before I pulled myself out of the house, through the wind, walking straight ahead until I found the Adepts dead as well, a circle of corpses at the edge of the reservation.

The adults behind me could not save me. Our guardians could not. So I did the only thing that made sense.

Empty and wholly alone, I stepped over their cold line.

Chapter 2

We have no reliable data for the numbers of the displaced over this five- year upheaval we now call the Great Reckoning. Rather than hunkering down, entire populations seemed to be on the move as if restlessness or a kind of unplanned pilgrimage could stop the changes their children experienced from within. That is the way of humans—to seek outside when the answers in their own hearts are silent.

Spirit Marga Census
Great Reckoning Archives

I don't know how long I walked those first few days. It was so very cold, that late autumn. I hadn't thought to bring a coat, or food for that matter. I lucked into a small reservation cabin the evening of the second day, empty of people, but with the heat cells and food storage units all functioning adequately. I remember staring into the bedrooms for a long time, chewing listlessly on a food bar, considering the pillows and the dusty comforters. In the end, I couldn't bring myself to creep into those empty beds. I curled up on the thick carpet, relatively warm and with a full belly, and stared at the walls until I finally slept.

In the morning, I set out walking again, trudging the rough two-track road, dressed in a heavy winter coat a size too large for me, following the path downward into the valley. It wasn't long before I could hear heavy machinery, and by early evening, I caught the faint glow of artificial lights in the sky. All too soon, the heavier darkness of the night descended again as the terrain shifted, and I found myself huddled between the roots of an old cedar for shelter.

And that is when I heard crying. It came softly, rhythmically, like someone rocking in time with the cries. I got up and followed the sound, my hands out in front of me, my feet shuffling through forest debris and stone.

I found her tangled in blackberry overgrowth, her face dirty and blond hair matted with leaves and bits of thorn. She'd torn the skin across her small nose, and her blue eyes were wild. Calmly, I talked to her, simple phrases over and over until I could free her, then she collapsed into my arms. "You're dead like me," she said finally, through her tears. "Dead just like me." I rocked her, stunned by her words, not knowing what to say, only aware that the motion calmed her. Finally, she slept and later, so did I.

The next day, I woke with her curled under the protective shelter of my arm. I shook her awake, and tried to find out her name, but she had lapsed into a dazed silence. Taking her hand, we made our way back to the rough drive, our steps drawing us ever downward out of reservation land.

The path opened up onto a large, prefab settlement. I could see a brilliant red cross painted on the side of the gray metal building. "It's a hospital or refugee center. Come on." I pulled her after me, our feet sliding in the mud.

We peeked through the first set of doors into a mess hall of some kind. The clank of eating utensils and conversation filled the room and for a few moments our presence went unnoticed. Only gradually did a kind of silence fall across the mess, as first one then several sets of eyes turned towards us. We all looked at each other for a heartbeat, then the cry went up. "Normals! We got two normal kids here!" A white-jacketed man sprang to his feet, nearly upending his drink in his excitement.

"Oh, thank God!"

"But where did they come...".

"...the reservation lands...."

They were all on their feet then, smiles cracking their tired faces. The little girl pulled back suddenly, startled by the attention and sudden eruption of noise. I bent, putting my hands on her shoulders. "We're OK now..."

And then the wail, twenty voices in one, rasped out a note of horror and pain.

I drew back, terrified as they fell, bleeding from their noses and ears, food trays upended, tipping into one another, reaching for one another. It took only moments, and then silence pressed at us, and all I could see was the brilliant red pooling on the floor and speckling those still, white coats. I stood there in shock, hardly blinking, barely feeling the small hand in mine. She tugged then, and I looked down at her. "I told you we were dead," she said softly. "I told you."

The alarms began their insistent wail from deeper in the complex.

CHAPTER 3

How do you counsel parents who are now the keepers of life forms they no longer recognize as their own children? How do you keep the human from turning violently against the Other, an inbred and dare we say natural reaction? And the greater question—when will those who no longer look human realize that they are in many ways smarter, faster, and more adept at survival than those who sometimes persecute them? The answer is that we must keep these children as children, dependent upon us, before they understand their own strength and so infuse the public with the idea that they are the very face of God that any who would hurt them will fear the wrath of the entire Spirit Marga. And as special people, as victims, the Children of God are dependent upon us.

Priest Psychologist
Spirit Marga
Archives

"Come on!" I yelled, jerking her back through the mess hall door. A cold rain had started to fall, and fog had descended on the hospital base. We ran parallel to the gray structure, aiming for the trees that might offer protection. Nobody emerged to give chase.

She was so small, her thin legs much shorter than mine. I fairly dragged her along the newly graveled yard. We angled out into the open finally, squinting against the rain, listening for the sound of pursuing feet. The forest lurked dark and absolutely still, as if watching us with dispassion.

In my head, a strange pinging had started, like a metal screw being dropped onto a ceramic plate. I blinked rapidly as we ran, my free hand occasionally reaching up to my ear as if that would stop the noise. Our feet slipped and stumbled on the loose stone, but finally we made it to the cover of the forest. The alarms screamed behind us, our breath came out in silvered clouds. The forest floor dropped away and we plunged over the edge of a steep embankment, scrambling over downed tree trunks and ducking the bare branches that whipped by our faces. Through the noise in my head, I could dimly hear her crying for me to stop, her small fingers clawing at my grip on her wrist. But the dead faces drove me on, faster and deeper into the woods.

She threw herself at me at last, her weight sending me down into the soaking leaves. We rolled hard, clear to the way to the bottom of the hill. I tried to rise, but my breath had been knocked out of me, and I fell again. She had scuttled away, making herself small beneath the edge of an enormous deadfall. Through the clinging ferns and moss, she stared at me, her bottom lip quivering.

I forced myself to sit still, my chest heaving, spots in my vision. The insistent pinging in my head had grown to a headache, monstrous. Then I could taste it, the salty and metallic taste of blood on my lips. I reached instinctively to my nose, and touched the sticky mess there. I could feel it trickling from my ears as the headache pressed inward. I reached out a hand toward her. "Stop," I pleaded. "Please don't. I'm sorry. I didn't mean to scare you."

She crept out, tears brimming her blue eyes. "Don't leave me dead," she cried. "Don't leave me, don't leave me, don't leave me." Her cries were not so much panicked as monotonous, a

kind of mantra. How many times had she said it?
And to how many dead faces?

I saw it all in her eyes, the horror and the
death. And then, something shifted in a wave of
nausea. It was as if I stood inside her. I felt the
curve of the vessels in her heart and brain. I
could feel her muscles working as she crept
closer. And in that moment, I began to
understand why I wasn't dead. Because as
something in me reached into her, I could feel
something of her reaching into me, holding back,
not quite ready to kill. But in that hesitation, I
understood how she did it, felt the intimacy of
her tiny life beating and how terribly fragile she
was. For one moment, I was she, and she was I.
One.

Above us, I could hear others coming after us
as I knew they would. Adult footfalls on damp
branches and undergrowth, the murmur of
communication units, the pinging growing
louder and her great blue eyes, glistening with
tears. In a moment, they would drop down the
hill and she would kill them and she didn't even
know how she did it. Because they were
protecting her, her nanotech within, saving their
tiny host in a way far beyond her own volition.

"I'm sorry," I said. I reached out, feeling myself within her and cut through the web of blood vessels in her brain.

It happened so fast. She looked startled for a moment, then her eyes glazed, rolled upward and she fell across my legs, dead.

The nanotech within her slammed into me. I cried out, writhing, my hands clutching my head, her weight partially holding my legs to the ground. And then, as suddenly as it had come, the assault passed. I could feel them swirl within me, integrating with me, flowing into the darkness of their new host. Becoming me. I opened my eyes to the darkness, and looked at what I had done.

Her eyes stared out into darkness, her skin so very white against my legs. I sobbed then, and gathered her against me, her wet and tangled hair soft against my cheek, and waited for the bullets to come from the darkness.

I was ten years old. I was a killer. And in those days of my own shock and fear, I hadn't even had the presence of mind to ask again for her name.

CHAPTER 4

*Many mistakes were made in the early years
of the Great Reckoning, mistakes having a
great deal to do with fear and a simple lack of
personnel training and resources. Without
understanding how to do the work of
integrating the new beings into society,
enforced deep sleep storage became the band-
aid of choice for those working with the more
dangerous manifestations of the Children of
God. But how the very designation of
"dangerous" was interpreted over wide
geographical areas remains, in the final
analysis, an even greater tragedy.*

*Notes from the Reckoning
Sociological Services Archives*

The search party from the medical
encampment emerged from the shadows like
wraiths, guns at ready, steps careful in the
undergrowth. They stopped in a ragged circle
around me, breathing through filters in a chorus
of forced exhales. I could feel their attention

tipped toward one of their own, even as they watched me

"Is she dead?" a slender one asked. Her voice, distorted by the filters, was cold.

I could taste my tears on my lips, mixing with the dried blood. I looked away, unable to speak at all. My head dropped as the sobs started again. Racking sobs. And they waited, none moving in the cold rain. I had never felt so guilty. Or so alone.

The slim figure shouldered her weapon and crouched carefully beside me. "I am senior staffer Medelia, a priest of the Spirit Marga." Her voice was softer now. "What was her name?"

"I don't know," I finally managed to choke out.

"*Your* name then. Come on son, just a name." I could feel the others shift nervously. I couldn't make out the features of her face. It occurred to me then, that she seemed able to study me just fine through her filtered mask and thin eye protection.

"Ianto," I said at last.

"Ianto, you're bleeding from your nose and ears. Did she do that to you?"

I nodded, the tears hot against my face.

"Would she have done that to us?" Medelia asked.

Again I nodded.

"No way, not with our gear," one male voice hissed. Medelia glanced his way, and he fell silent.

"What killed her, Ianto?" she asked.

I let her question hang in the forest and rain. I felt like a wild creature, gone to ground, but surrounded. I could fight or surrender, but even as a ten-year-old, I knew the one thing they must not learn was the truth.

"She just fell. She was killing me and she just fell. She just fell and I caught her." I let myself dissolve in tears again. That felt good, to let the fear and anger and loneliness break open.

Medelia rose slowly to her feet. She gestured for two of the larger men to pick up the little girl's body. They did so carefully, watching me cry. Wordlessly, they slipped her into a black bag. I noticed, with a thrill of horror that they had two; perhaps they had not expected to take either of us alive.

Medelia looked down on me, her hands still cradling her weapon. "I have to put you in a stasis bag, Ianto. We'll take you back to the field hospital and put you in isolation for a while. To protect you, and to protect the people who are trying to help you get better. Do you understand?"

I eyed the bag that held the little girl. Her form barely expanded its cover. I could hear the men shifting again, ready to use force. We are dead, she had said.

"I'm so tired." I looked up at Medelia's black faceplate.

"I can help you with that," she murmured kindly.

CHAPTER 5

In the end, the Mercy was inevitable. Later generations may try to intellectually disprove this simple statement, but they did not live in our times, did not see what some of the Children of God had become. The very fact that unaltered humans are still left alive to criticize anything may not occur to them. And it is equally likely they will not understand the value of the scapegoat to stabilize a critical political climate.

Science Marga Analyst
Understanding The Mercy

I woke to sunlight cutting a swath across my bed. I followed the beams with my eyes, to the narrow light source set along the ceiling level. The back wall of the tiny room was gray, but the other three walls were glass. Beyond my cell, I could see a long row of beds and machinery and rooms like my own.

For a moment I was disoriented, but then I remembered the rain, being zipped into darkness with cloth enfolding me, the faceplates a blank circle all around me.

So this is where I had been taken.

I sat up cautiously, pushing against sheets pulled too tightly across my arms and chest. Now I could make out the little computer stations, set in gentle curves along the row of cells, and techs bent over their instrumentation.

But something was wrong. I looked at my hands. They were big, long fingered, clean with evenly cut nails. I held my arms out, looking at their impossible size. Then I touched my face. The bones were all wrong, the lips wider, the cheeks higher than they should have been. I dropped my hands immediately, nauseated, but then forced myself out of the bed, my bare feet cold on the metal floor. The loose pants whispered against my legs. In two awkward strides I was where the door should have been, and splayed my new fingers against the glass. Seamless. Cold.

Ping, Ping, Ping. The sound echoed in my head. I glanced up and to my left. A small gray triangle nestled in the junction of ceiling, two walls. "Stop," I murmured to it. The ping quieted almost at once. I blinked, surprised. I had not expected the machine to actually listen to me, and I might have grinned then at the absurdity of it.

One of the techs whirled at his station. His eyes narrowed when he saw me. I wasn't sure what to do, so I waved a little, my head tipped to the side. Even waving felt strange. I liked him immediately, though. His blond hair and height reminded me of my Viking adept. He mumbled into his lapel mike, his eyes never leaving mine. I waved a little again, trying out the motion, and felt oddly satisfied at his still stunned expression.

Then, all the techs were turning, but not to look at me. I angled my head to try to see where their attention had been drawn.

She entered with a retinue, all of them dressed in flowing blue robes. Spirit Marga, elite priests. I knew the look from my childhood. Some had pulled their hoods up to conceal their faces, but she did nothing to hide her long black hair and deep brown eyes. "Who is in charge of this facility?" Her voice was slightly muffled by the walls of my cell, but I could make out her words well enough.

My Viking tech stepped forward, extending his hand. "Senior biotech Willin. How can I help you, Your Grace?"

She looked at the hand for a moment then finally shook with him. "God be with you. My name is Jean Molair. I have been sent with the appropriate signed documentation to inform you that the Spirit Marga has purchased this facility. I will need your protocols for a final shut down and decommissioning. I have transports waiting for your team."

I could see the panic run through the techs. No, I corrected myself. Not panic - horror.

"But," Willin stammered. "These are still our children. We can't just..."

"Can't just what?" Her face went cold. "They are the most dangerous Children of God, tech Willin. We are sending them to their spiritual home and we shall hold the responsibility for their deaths before they become fully the monsters you already know them to be." Her voice dropped, but her eyes remained resolute. "We are saving their souls. Because it is the *only* thing we can do for them."

She gestured at her people, who fanned out along the corridor of glass and terminals. The biotechs stepped out of their way, their eyes seeking Willin for guidance. I splayed both hands against the glass, trying to make some kind of sense of the world around me, of my new body, of the woman who commanded with such ease.

And then she looked directly at me, her eyes wide, her lips open.

CHAPTER 6

Doubt is the most powerful change machine of all the religious feelings. It is a lightening bolt that wakes us up, even when it takes the guise of emptiness or restlessness or mere boredom. Doubt is a shift of mind, a renewal of responsibility, a harbinger of a wider world of the possible.

Sermon 42
Head Priest, Old York

I watched her cross slowly to my cell, her face solemn. She gently touched the glass and I felt the ripple of her fingers as if on my own skin. She was reading something on her side, posted where I could not see it. I realized, in that moment, how much taller I had grown, because even though she was an adult, her head only reached my shoulder. That made me dizzy, almost nauseated, like everything around me had shrunk and distanced itself from me.

She finally looked up and the watery sheen of her dark eyes startled me.

"I'm sorry. You weren't supposed to be awake. None of you were supposed to be awake."

I struggled to understand what that might mean, but mostly it was her tears that began to frighten me.

"I've just read your file, Ianto. You've been designated as one of the dangerous Children of God; they say you might have killed an entire emergency hospital staff and later a little girl," she said.

"No. It wasn't me," I answered her. The sound came out garbled and scratched. I put my hand and forehead against the glass. My legs shook. I saw her stiffen, saw her want to step back. But she didn't.

"I wish we knew for sure. Truly. What I find myself struggling with is that after five years in a controlled coma, you wake up today, at just this time, just when we arrive." Her dark eyes looked directly into mine. "I'm not trained to believe anything is really an accident, you see."

Five years. I looked at the hands that were not my own, then back into her face.

"Please understand. I have been ordered to terminate this facility to protect the populations beyond these walls. If I could, I would set you free. But I am bound to obey my orders."

"No," I murmured. My voice sounded terrible, too deep and low in my throat. "You have to let me out. I'm not...I'm not *dangerous!*" My heart was starting to thunder in my chest, and trickles of sweat coursed down my sides.

"We are calling it the Mercy." She laughed then, a bitter and self-contained sound as if she didn't hear my pleading. "Though whom it is a mercy for will be debated for some time. In fifteen minutes I am going to flood these floors with a deadly gas. Twenty minutes after that, the whole place will be fired and the levels collapsed one on top of another. The entire structure will be filled in and capped with a beautiful memorial. After all, the people must have their place to lay their flowers and light their candles."

She looked straight into my eyes and her gaze was abruptly sharp and brilliant. "Still. If it is God's will, you can get out. Come to me at the west entrance." She pointed down the long stretch of hall to her right. "I will wait at the tree line until we fire the building, and then I will leave. But I cannot open this door. The protocols for this event have already been set in motion. Do you understand?"

I cast around my room, looking for door relays, or something with enough heft to break the glass. I threw myself against the divider, and this time she did step back, her lip line hard.

"I don't know how!" I cried. "Help me!"

"This thing is in God's hands." She turned, gathering her priests around her, ushering the remaining techs toward the doors.

"Don't!" I screamed against the glass. "NO!"

And then techs and monks were gone and I stared like a captured fish at an empty and sterile world.

CHAPTER 7

God, in our society, has become an idea so
vast and impersonal that we have found
ourselves orphaned. I recall when my mother
said one of the names of God was Al-Wakil,
the Guardian. I nearly collapsed in a heap of
grateful tears. For days, I went about feeling
hands on my shoulders, and aware of my own
private protector. I was safe. I was guarded
by something breathing and alive within me.
Something powerful and tangible. Today, I
wish I could pull that guardian out of my
subconscious and share him with all these
broken souls. Oh, to be sure the God of our
high philosophy is just, broad and awesome.
But if God cannot place you under the shadow
of his wings, the poetry of this life begins to
grow stale.

A God for the Reckoning
Merryl Lee

I pounded again and again at the glass until
the skin split across the edges of my hand. My
breath rang back to me, four walls reflecting the

sound, amplifying it. Crying in frustration, I knit my fingers into my hair and fell sobbing, sliding down the wall. My body was not my own; too big, too weak, and I could smell my own sweat.

"Momma," I cried finally, gulping at the air and rocking myself. "Momma." I could feel the minutes ticking down, trickling down, asleep for years and now soon dead to gas and fire and a gray capstone where living parents could come and lay their flowers.

No one would lay flowers for me.

"God," I cried, a last strangling desperation. "Help me."

I had never talked to God much, even though my mother and I were members of the Spirit Marga. She was quiet about her faith, aside from what I saw and heard of her meditation, dances, chanting. She did not teach me in so many words. God to me had been the light on pine needles, the smell of the earth, the way a deer stopped and watched me from a ridge away. God was hugs and hot cocoa, even rain, even tears after a skinned knee.

"Please. God."

I knelt at the glass, my hands and forehead flat against it, praying, my breath fogging the surface. I could feel the glass, warming to my touch, the way the molecules fit together, and the space, so much space between. Reality could be felt. Space, more than sensed, could be stroked and bathed in. God did hear. And then I was falling forward, through the wall and onto the floor beyond. I hit hard, the breath knocked out me for a moment. I looked up the glass wall, at the oval cut perfectly where I had crouched.

And then I was on my feet in that awful silence, stumbling and clumsy in the broken glass, piloting a body that no longer felt like my own. I felt the metal grating cut into my bare feet, but the pain was distant, vaguely unreal. I flung myself toward the west entrance, toward the tree line beyond, where at least one living being said she would wait for me.

I don't remember saying thank-you to whatever had heard me. But then, perhaps the thanks echoed in my breath.

CHAPTER 8

The Northwest Monastery system was built a century prior to the great plagues that ravaged the world. It served as a hospital and a place of retraining in small-scale agriculture, a library and a haven for those who had lost their entire families. As such, it more closely echoed its religious roots than the larger Spirit Marga, which, by design, included psychologists, sociologists, artists, teachers, architects and healers. And yet, splinters of all those other fields continue to echo in each monk, according to his or her gifts.

Understanding the Monastic System
of the Spirit Marga
A First Primer

At the tree line, true to her word, she was waiting. The sky was still tinged red with the last of evening color as I stumbled to her side. She looked up at me for a long while and then, with a nod, beckoned me to follow. We skirted the edge of the woods then walked across a vast parking lot of artificial light and wet pavement. Even though it was mostly empty now, I could hear the soft whir of vehicles moving on the other side of the building. She spoke into the air about charges, the placement of the final cap, and paused every so often, listening. She completely ignored me until we got to a small two-seated electric vehicle. Still talking to others I could not see, she opened the door, and gestured me inside to the passenger seat.

I huddled there, my spine curving into the plastic seat, shaking. My mind was blank, my world limited to the dust on her dashboard.

After a time, she entered the car. Sitting behind the wheel, she leaned her head back and closed her eyes. "Three thousand children in this facility. So many facilities all over the world. All sealed tonight. God help us." I turned to look at her, warily. Did she know that God heard such things? And then, in the gathering darkness, she started to cry. Not loudly. Not with racking sobs, just a slow drizzle of tired tears. Even when the ground trembled violently beneath us, rocking our car, she sat unmoving, eyes closed around her secret misery.

I can remember sitting there, outside of time. I thought perhaps she had fallen asleep, but finally, she turned her head toward me. "You got out. Somehow, I knew you could. You woke up. It was a sign from God. But beyond that I have no idea what to do with you." In the parking lot lights, she looked harsher somehow, older, her eyes shadowed, her lips a thin line.

I had no words to offer her.

Finally, she straightened, and put her transport into gear. We drove through the parking lot and the dense fog that I dimly realized must be dust from the collapsed facility. Then we were out on a forest road, the trunks of trees spinning past in her headlights.

We drove all night in silence. I didn't know if she was purposefully dallying or if we had an actual destination. I wasn't hungry, wasn't thirsty, and wasn't tired. I just stared straight ahead, watching the ribbon of road unfolding.

Finally, we stopped before a massive gate, and she spoke quickly into the darkness. The gate slid back obediently, and we wound around a narrow paved road until we stopped at a small parking lot. It was empty, except for us. "Come on, Ianto."

I stepped out on the cement, wincing as the pavement nipped at my broken and tender feet. She moved away, following a little gray path with tiny solar lights along its edges. I hobbled behind her, occasionally glancing around into the deeper pools of darkness, then the edge of this plant, the way the small lights shimmered.

An imposing wall of stone loomed up and we found ourselves before another gate, this one designed for foot traffic. It rose into the night, high and narrow with a delicate arch. Again, the whispered words, and again the gate sighed away. We entered a walled garden, not very big, and beyond hunkered a small house with a red door, its walls illuminated in a soft glow of solar path lights. She opened the house door, and asked in an almost-whisper for the interior lights to come up.

I crept forward cautiously, pausing in the doorway. She had already opened up the restroom so I could see in. She gestured with her head, "Shut the door. It's getting cold."

It was a simple place, kitchen off to the left, bed to the right, a little desk under the front window, restroom straight ahead. She got down on her knees and lifted the bedcover, exposing a neat row of built-in cabinets. She opened one, and pulled out a green robe and something else, placing them neatly on top of the black bedspread. She stood then, her fingers interlaced in front of her, considering me.

"These are the robes and a full hood of a hermit of the Spirit Marga. I've logged you in under a high authorization, and nobody will make you leave. This is a kind of sanctuary for you if you choose to stay. All the Children of God are welcome. Your abbot is Hobert, a good man, a kind man. There is a food unit in the kitchen, and the bath at your disposal. Do you understand?"

I nodded mutely.

"The hood will give you privacy. You can choose to use it or not. Hobert will stop in and check on you in the morning. You can treat your feet with the flesh sealant in the restroom—I noticed you were limping as you came in. There is a text access pad in the desk drawer. You can read I assume?"

I nodded again, not quite willing to speak. She must have seen my eyes casting about, the flush of fear on my cheeks.

"No one will harm you here, Ianto. You have my word."

I looked into her dark eyes. "Thank you," I said at last.

She cocked her head slightly, her dark eyes considering me then finally she tipped her head. "Get some rest. Morning will come soon."

Moments later, I stood alone in a hermitage of the Spirit Marga.

CHAPTER 9

If the plagues and the Great Reckoning took much from human civilization, the one thing it gave back to us all was time. It was like the tyranny of more, faster, better dissolved in tears, rusted in the emptying cities, and some of us discovered the sky, and the smell of the land, and how the way rain streaming on the window can be blessed and good.

Essays from Interesting Times
An Anthology of Views

I suppose the life of a monk is not exactly what a teenager might consider a dream existence. But for me, the rhythm of the days had a beauty and predictability that soothed me. It was not that I didn't play with the idea of other lives, of very real passion or different paths I could take in the world, but rather, when I deeply considered those avenues, I felt a kind of weariness in my bones.

Hobert, the abbot of the Northwest Monastery, proved to be a good man, a gentle man, even when I repeatedly rebuffed his invitations to speak more deeply about myself. Even though I had chosen the full hood, consigning myself to a world cut up of mesh lines and muffled sound, he never pushed me to shed it. His greatest gift to me was gently bringing me into the choir, where the ancient chants from our founding traditions echoed against the plain high stone walls of the meeting hall. I had a sweet enough voice, I suppose. Not as lilting as the Sea Children's tones, nor as deep and resonant as what the Were's could manage, but certainly serviceable.

And of course I read, deep into the night, the entire world's scripture made available to me. And learned the discipline of meditation. And worked in my garden, replaying the years of reservation living through my hands and the soil. Hobert chided me for working in the full habit sometimes, but I took it as the gentle teasing it was.

At night, I lay awake in my hermitage after reading nearly until dawn, and did not often sleep. I told no one about this little quirk, as it did not bother me over much and certainly harmed no one else. I took to sending my mind out into the walls of my little home, then further a field, into roots and out into branches where at least the breeze rocked me. My world had grown large with time, and breathed through me. I ached occasionally to talk with someone about the wonder of it all, but ended up keeping such things to myself. Looking back, I know it offered me a kind of security like the hood of my habit.

They tried to set up surveillance around my small property, but I always felt the technological intrusion, the echoing ping deep in my skull. And something in me reached out and broke it all. I didn't speak of it and they did not ask. If they were afraid of me, they showed no sign.

And so the years passed, uneventful, quiet, with Hobert's unobtrusive presence and the silent companionship of the other monks. I grew taller still, although I stayed slender, and after bathing I would sometimes study my face in the mirror. My eyes had changed color -- they were almost an aquamarine tone and startling against my deep brown eyebrows and tousled hair. My face had taken on a gaunt look, with sharp cheekbones but a strong jaw. I still watched for signs of the Great Reckoning, the physical changes that would come and turn me into a monster, but my fear began to lessen with each passing year. On the outside at least, I could still pass as human.

I had seen some of my fellow monks working in the sun, shed of their habits. Some of their variations made me cringe at first; I will not recount them here because whole libraries are full of what we children had become. Here and there, an older monk worked alongside these terrible ones, clapped them on the back, and laughed with them.

I could not do that, not yet.

So if I kept to my monk's hood and habit, it was because I did not want them to see my face or my fear. Both, in their way, shamed me. Until I could move around them with such casual ease, I would stay hidden. They deserved that from me, or at least that was the excuse I had become comfortable with.

Chapter 10

One of the first things we began to observe
with no small sense of foreboding was that
the Children of God had very little of what we
would call self-will. They tended to gravitate
to outside control in a uniform way no human
society had ever exhibited, particularly when
they functioned in groups. Early sociological
studies chalked this up to excessive pleasing
behaviors, or their discomfort with their own
sense of difference outside their own cohort,
but over time, others in the field began to
posit that most seemed to share some sort of
common inner bond. It was like they moved
to a kind of inner drone-note that unaltered
humans couldn't quite hear. The
discomforting thought arose. Who was
playing that one note that hummed through
them all?

Psychology of the Children of God
Andre DeFlannery

Jean came to stay with us, early in my third
year, as a resident at the monastery. Her

presence awoke memories in me, bitter things that clutched at my gut, and so I tried very hard to avoid her. For a while, she honored this, leaving space between us when we sang together, leaving the field if we happened to work too closely.

One day, I was weeding in my personal garden. The clouds had gathered, and thunder rumbled. I looked up, and she was standing there at my gate, patient, waiting for me to see her. I hesitated for a moment before I beckoned her in.

In my time at the monastery, I had learned that if I kept myself very still, people could not read me at all. There was no face to observe, no body language if I controlled myself. I stood, brushing the debris from my knees, then bowed at the waist.

"Welcome," I said. Ah, but the voice. My voice was still not always mine to control when my mind was running too fast. Today, it crackled around the edges a bit.

She smiled, sadly it seemed to me. "Ianto. It has been a long time since we have spoken. You'll forgive the intrusion, but Hobert and Cyntia have asked I begin to meet with you, each day, as your director. I know my presence makes you nervous, but we must get past that now."

I considered her through the mesh of my habit. "I did not request a director," I answered.

She smiled again, this time with a wry twist at her lips. "I know." She gestured to one of the stone benches that lined my wall. "So I will sit, and when you want to talk with me, I will be here, at this time every day."

The thunder rumbled again.

"In the rain?" I asked her.

"Unless you choose to invite me in," she replied.

For a moment, I was very tempted to let her sit there with lightning flashing around her and possibly hail falling on her head. The thought amused me a little, but finally, picking up my fresh basket of weeds, I indicated with my head for her to follow. By the time I had dumped my load onto the compost pile, the drops were falling hard and fast. We escaped indoors, she laughing under her breath in delight.

I took a seat on the edge of my bed, while she pulled out my study chair. She glanced around, her quick eyes catching the details of my small home, her face still flushed from our race with the rain.

"Would you like tea?" I asked. I thought, with a great deal more interest than a monk should have, how lovely her dark hair moved when free and loose, her waist outlined tight with her belt. But then the old memories pressed, things I did not want to remember, so I looked away.

"No, I'll pass on the tea because you can't join me dressed in that," she said, pointing to my hood.

I stayed perfectly still.

"Ianto," she said, leaning forward at her waist. "You have lived among us now for years, and we have fed you and given you a home. It's time to choose a vocation whereby you can begin to repay that debt."

"Funny. I thought by taking me in, the Spirit Marga was repaying a debt owed to me and all the Children of God," I answered her.

"You will grow tired of simply accepting hospitality. You need a purpose." She stressed that final word with her perfectly pitched voice.

"God is not enough of a purpose?" I returned. I was growing very quickly to like this conversation, particularly as the color came up strong on her cheeks.

"You know it is not enough to know God; you must serve others, Ianto, or your understanding of our way is imperfect."

"As the Children of God are imperfect." I smiled smugly.

"You see them that way, I don't, " she retorted, with a firm shake of her head.

She had me there. My head dropped a little, and I could see she understood her jab had found its mark.

"Ianto, I think I know why you continue to wear the hood. Unless you have greatly changed since I saw you last, you would not look like most of the children here."

"We are not children anymore," I answered, irritation creeping into my voice. I hated her in that moment, hated that she could see through me with such ease.

"Yes you are. All of you. Hurt children, children still bleeding. And if you do not begin to turn your minds to a purpose, you will begin to crumble." She abruptly sat up straighter, hands gripping her own knees. "We have counselors here, but you don't go. We have the abbot and other elder monks and priests to speak with, but you do not seek them out for anything other than banter. We have groups that meet and talk and you give them a wide circle. So now, you have me. Everyday."

I looked down at my dirty habit, trying to make my hands relax against the fabric. "We'll run out of words very quickly," I said.

"Then I will sit here for the appointed hour and share the silence with you," she replied. To my consternation, she closed her eyes and prepared to do just that.

Chapter 11

*At first, we were secure in the knowledge that
the nanotech required biological systems to
sustain their own functionality; that we were
somehow superior to them, the ground of
their being so to speak. We were once again
too shortsighted to realize how we all
function as part of ever larger and more
complex systems. We did not understand that
eventually we would be the ones who could
not exist without the bits of technology
swirling in the leaves, in our animals, in the
marrow of our very bones. There could not be
a "them" and an "us". And when we awoke to
this fact, it was like when humankind looked
up into the stars for the first time and felt
suddenly very small.*

And What Now is Humankind?
Terce McNammara

Jean lay back on the green grass, gazing up
into the network of autumn leaves. The sun
caught their brilliant edges and the breeze every
so often whisked a handful away from their

branches. I lay beside her, my finger twirling one leaf stem slowly, slowly, nodding round and round.

"So you are telling me you can feel the inside of this tree?" Jean rolled her head to look at me.

"All of it, from the roots to the top branches," I answered. "Better when I can touch it, but yes, I can feel it even inside my hermitage."

"How do you know you aren't just imagining it?" she asked.

"How do you know when you have touched the face of God?" I returned.

"I haven't yet, that's how," and she laughed then, lighthearted.

I smiled behind my mask. In that moment, I wanted to pull the hood aside, and look full into her face. I regretted the months of silence, and then months more of cat and mouse conversation I had inflicted upon her. Someday I would say I was sorry. Someday.

"So how do you prove such a thing?" she asked.

I considered the tree. I felt my mind moving in the veins of the old oak, felt the wind tugging at the leaves as if they were strands of my own hair. "There, I said. "See that leaf with the big hole in it? Part of it is still greenish?"

She cast around a bit then finally said she had found it.

"Tell me when you want it to break loose," I said.

"OK." She waited for a long time, her eyes on the leaf. Then, in a flash, when the wind was at its most still, she told me to do it.

And the leaf dropped off the branch, falling straight to the ground not far from her feet.

She sat up, and for one moment, the look she gave me was wide eyed and startled. I came up from the ground slowly, to sit beside her. I think she might even have drawn back, but then something in her steeled.

"Do it again," she said.

So I did. Four more times in fact, although with each leaf, I felt my stomach growing a little heavier. We sat for a while in silence after the last one tumbled to earth.

"What else can you feel into, Ianto?" she asked at last.

"You know the answer to that," I said. "You knew when you found me and you knew when I joined you by the woods that night. I can feel inside anything, everyone."

"And make it all fall down, like a leaf from a tree?"

"Yes," I said. I understood, then, the notion of a broken heart. I hurt in my chest, like a giant hand was pressed against me. "And now," I said with no little amount of bitterness and self-loathing, "you are afraid of me."

She reached out then, her hand against the side of my hood, her eyes trying to reach through the mesh into my own. "No, Ianto. You are Spirit Marga, and if you had wanted to hurt any of us, you would have already. I alone have certainly provoked you enough, yet here I am, sitting with you. I am amazed and troubled by your gift, but I'm not afraid."

I nodded, shrugging off her touch gently.

"So, now I think you want to come to it," Jean said softly.

"Come to what?" I asked.

"The little girl in the woods, the one mentioned in the Marga files...what happened?" she asked softly. She put her hand on my shoulder then, and I wanted so badly to lean into her. The wind pulled her hair across her face, but her eyes stayed steadily on me.

Memories. Awful, bloody memories. I found myself saying, "she would have killed me...not her, they..." then stopped. Jean squeezed my shoulder gently. I shut my eyes then, but couldn't hide. "I ...I don't know how, but in that act she shared something with me. I could see into her, her mind, and the nanotech and the whole thing that she was. So afraid and so angry and so alone. And when I heard others coming, I could feel what would happen. So I...I ..." At first, the tears choked me but I wouldn't let them out. "I didn't know what else to do." And then something in me broke open and I was falling down against her shoulder, neck straining against the sobs that ripped through me.

"You saved them," Jean said softly after a time, holding me so very carefully and so very solidly. "You saved them all, except that one little girl who you could not save, Ianto. And they, no, we, thanked you by stealing five years of your life."

"No." I shoved myself back from her. "I didn't kill all of her. Don't you see? She is still here, in me. I became her; it lives in me, her talent. I feel everything. Everyone. It's right here." I knit my fingers in my hood at my temple, the cloth bunching. "I'm terrified it will happen again. That I'll kill again. That's why I don't want to have a purpose here. I just want to live apart, live quietly. I can't...." My voice broke off, the silence taking up space where I had left off.

Jean considered me a moment, then shook her head. Her eyes were wide and compassionate. "Oh, Ianto," she sighed at last. "Don't you see? You are not an undisciplined and terrified four-year old. You are not she."

Chapter 12

It has always been important to keep the Emperium in the background, a kind of stupid second cousin, a mindless servant. But of course, we know they employ minds no less brilliant than our own. Our greatest fear is that, in spite of their inbred emphasis on short-range plans and rapid implementation of hot-zone social control, they will stumble into real power one day. That is something we cannot allow.

Notes on the Emperium
Anthony Stelle, Sixth Executive,
Science Marga

My studies were going well, the garden flourished and my hour each day with Jean was something I had grown to treasure. She brought less spiritual things to me; novels and electronic palm games and chocolate, new music and images from beyond the monastery of great underground cities and flat oceans undisturbed by any boat. We talked a great deal about the world beyond my walls and her friendship was easy, her humor infectious. And if the day of trees and falling leaves and sorrow really had frightened her, she gave me no sign.

I was nineteen now, a teen growing into a man. And sometimes, I could even sleep in the small hours of the morning, three or four hours at a stretch.

The midday meal was taken in community most days, in a hall with soaring walls and clear windows chased with sunlight. Eating without conversation, our space fluttered and chimed with the presence of two hundred Children of God. I sat beside Jean, my hands folding occasionally across my chest to say "no thank you" to the proffered dishes.

She leaned close to me, wickedly wagging her fork just beyond my mask. The potato smelled like heaven. I kicked her playfully sideways beneath the table and her shoulders shook with silent mirth. I was happy enough that day, sun seeping across the tabletops and flooring, the gray walls alight and golden, the big silver trays steaming on the tables, the drink passing from hand to what now served as a hand.

But weather sometimes changes in minutes. One moment, sunshine, the next, storm scudding clouds ripping across the skies.

Jean was one of the first to go, her hands suddenly gripping the table top, her open-mouthed surprise turning so quickly to a stare. I caught her as she sagged against me. Like a wave, the Children of God fell, over the tables, or slipped sideways and fell to the floor. Glasses shattered, silverware rang on the stones, all of it a great din for a moment before a perfect silence. The sunlight seemed a thing alive, dancing with dust motes, the only thing moving in the great hall.

I struggled with Jean's body, laying her awkwardly on the floor, my hands searching frantically for a pulse. And when I found it, I nearly collapsed in relief.

Then they came, through the doors on each side of the hall, soldiers in gray uniforms sprayed into the dining hall. I dropped swiftly to the floor. One man, striking with his short-cropped black hair and tangible confidence, fanned his men out with simple hand gestures. "Find him. Use your bio scanners."

They broke up, each man or woman to a table, their small hand-helds sweeping over each unconscious Child of God.

I felt the pings then, many of them, metallic gravel dropped on a tabletop. And I did what I had always done; I reached out and broke them.

Murmurs of surprise went up. Here a man shook his unit, there another tapped at the blank screen. The commander merely smiled tightly. "We have him, then. He's here. And he's awake."

The words sunk in far too fast. They knew me, what I could do. I had given myself away.

"Ianto. Stand up and show yourself." The soldier turned slowly in the great room, his black eyes sweeping details as they moved across the fallen bodies.

"What does he look like?" one man asked.

The commander shook his head, his hand snapping up, warning him to silence.

So they didn't know, or he recognized that I wore the full habit like a few other monks. Perhaps he didn't know what the Great Reckoning might have done to my body, my face. I lay beside Jean, breathing, my heart banging against my ribs, my mesh-shielded eyes watching the soldiers.

Boots walked by us, slowly. I could smell the man and feel the heat of tension radiating from him. The soldier stopped for a moment then moved on. They simply didn't know what they were looking for.

The commander considered for a moment. I saw him sigh as if what he was preparing to do would land him in no small amount of trouble. "There will be a normal woman here, long dark hair, blue habit. Find her, you will find him."

If I could have moved, I would have covered her with my body, but as it was, the boots that had walked by us spun, and the soldier flashed back to us. "Here!" He had a young man's voice, eager to please.

I held myself very still, a lifetime of practice. I heard the feet making their way toward us, a commander's step, firm and confident, even as he stepped over the fallen. Then he was squatting beside us, his elbows on his thighs, his hands hanging loose in front of him. "That's her."

He considered me a moment, then his eyes slid right and left. I didn't move.

He shifted then, and brought his pistol out. He tapped it against his palm, as if considering, then pointed it at Jean's temple. "Ianto, you will remand yourself to our custody now or I will pull this trigger."

In that moment, I felt the coldest of rages come over me. I could feel them, feel into all of them, the pulse of their blood, the electric fire-show of their minds. And I could have turned them off, one by one. I struggled with it, my eyes filled with the pistol almost touching Jean's forehead.

But Jean had told me I was not she, not a four-year old child lost and alone.

I sat up slowly, and to his credit the commander merely stood and took a measured step back, his gun snapping from Jean to me. I came to my feet, my open hands telling him I would not fight. We were eye-to-eye, so to speak, this soldier and I. I wanted to tell him how his heart beat in my head, how I could play at will in the tapestry of veins in his skull, but I kept my silence.

"Ianto of the Spirit Marga." He nodded, his face hard. "You are being taken into custody by order of the state. You will be remanded to a Northern Emperium facility until further notice."

I did not answer him; there was no need.

"What about her?" the young soldier asked.

"Any action that touched her would probably cost me my life."

His life? I dropped my eyes to Jean's unconscious form, confused.

When I looked up, the commander smiled a bit. "Didn't know, did you? She is the daughter of the High Priestess of the Spirit Marga, Cyntia Molair. You keep high company for a Child of God, Ianto. Of course, from what I know of you, you're dangerous enough to warrant a very short chain."

I swallowed, my brow knitting over my eyes almost to the point of pain. "I am a danger to no one," I finally said.

"Good." The commander gestured with his gun, "that way."

With one more look Jean, I stepped over her and walked through the silent hall, a pistol trained on my back.

Chapter 13

I wonder, sometimes, if our monks know they are bought and sold and accounted for each moment of their lives. Their vows are less important than the data they provide and the occasional chess piece they must become. In ages past, this management style might have seemed cold. But the value of the human being has always been in what can be bartered from its skills, concrete or otherwise. We are relational creatures after all.

Spirit Marga Yearly Report
Senior Analyst

They steered me through the sunlight to a military van, beckoning me up into the back of the transport. The doors were shut, locked, and I sat alone. In time we were swaying along, and I had to work to keep my balance on the low flat seats. Ugly seamed steel and bolts were the only feature, and so for a time, I simply hung on and nursed my confusion and frustration.

It was a long drive, and I was sore and tired by the time the van halted and the doors opened. The sunset, spectacular over the high wire fences, cast a red glow over the single-story buildings and dusty but meticulously parked vehicles. I looked around for a troop transport, but only the dark haired commander and one other man waited for me. "Ianto," the leader beckoned, and made way for me to drop to the gravel.

We entered a gray building, passed by an empty desk. I did not miss the dust settling on everything, or how many of the lights did not come on as we moved along. Our steps echoed down the long hallway to a utilitarian elevator shaft. I counted seven floors as we dropped into the earth and then the doors opened. The commander and his man stepped out into the brilliant light, but I hung back, shocked for a moment with memories.

A row of glass rooms stretched before me, running for the length of a football field at least, with tech stations set opposite of them every twenty feet or so. The commander, sensing my hesitation, stopped, turned back toward me and opened his hand. "Ianto."

In that moment, I ran through what it would take to close the elevator doors, to break it on the surface, buying me time to run. But run where?

The soldier pulled his gun, while the bare second or three flicked past. I turned my head toward him and in that moment I saw just how afraid of me he really was. It was a look I will always remember, a mind running in panic and all of it at play on his face.

Instead of breaking away or killing, I stepped cautiously back into my old nightmare.

Only after the elevator doors slid shut, did it dawn on me that the inhabitants of the glass cages were not sleeping. Some, near to the lift, stood as I came in. There, a man with wings folded across his back like an angel, and next to him, a huge woman with bony ridges running down her naked scalp and forehead in frozen waves that crashed and curled around her jaw line. Others, down the row, I could see less clearly. The Children of God considered the stranger standing in their midst, staring frankly at me, a monk from the Spirit Marga in my soft green habit and hood.

The commander took my elbow, and led me along the front of the clear quarters. Forty feet in, he steered me right, and we entered another hall of closed doors, long light bars illuminating its ceiling. These walls and portals were solid and metallic, though. We didn't go far before he released me to unlock one.

This time, he had me go in first, his shoulder close to mine. "Remain outside," he told the soldier who seemed more than eager to comply.

The room was painted in soft earth tones. My feet sunk into a rich carpet. Two deep chairs crouched by a gas fireplace off to my left, and to my right a simple bed and bathroom waited. "It was thought you might be more comfortable here. The nature of your escape from the Mercy is well known among our upper administration. I'm sorry if the cells started you at first glance."

"How could you know that?" I asked, turning toward the commander.

He chuckled, as he shut the door firmly. "You didn't get all the security cameras, you know. I've seen the footage myself, a kid falling right through a hole in the glass then running like hell. Made us upgrade the holding cells here, oscillate the crystalline structure. But in all truth it was probably a wasted effort; there is probably not another Child of God quite like you."

"What do you want with me?" I asked.

"We'll eat together and discuss that presently."

"Will you drug me with food like you did the entire dining hall?" I turned away from him, making my way to a chair where I sat down stiffly, on its edge.

He, on the other hand, flopped easily. The artificial lights made his hair almost blue. "I wondered why you didn't go down. Hard to eat through that mask, though, isn't it? So why do you go to the hall...some kind of penance or something?

"Only when they serve chocolate cake," I replied without missing a beat. "And this is a habit hood, not a mask."

He grinned. "Whatever. You won't be needing it here anymore."

"I'm a monk of the Spirit Marga, commander. Being here does not change that."

He considered me for a moment. "You're wrong. Being here changes everything, Ianto," he said softly. I could not miss the threat or pity in his voice.

Chapter 14

We knew the Children of God could be manipulated by outside sources, particularly through their nanotech connections. We simply did not know if such a fate could befall us all. And when we began to face that possibility, perhaps that eventuality, some of began to believe again in Hell.

Who's Mind?
Readings in Developmental Spirituality

His hand went up, calming me, the softened feature of his ancient face lifting into an affable smile. "Ianto, I am fine, fine."

I rounded on the commander. "What does this mean? How dare you take the abbot! If you wanted a war with the Spirit Marga, you could not have chosen a better way!" I tried to put every withering ounce of energy I could behind my words, but the dark haired soldier simply smiled, brushed past me, and clasped Hobert's hand.

"Abbot Hobert, it is done as you commanded." And he went to one knee, kissing the wrinkled knuckles. Hobert nodded, looking a little exasperated at such a show. As gracefully as he had bowed, the commander rose, the two men now looking at me a bit like two children sharing a secret between them.

"I thought..." I began.

The commander smiled. "As you were meant to. I am a monk of the Spirit Marga not unlike you, but perhaps with a different kind of training. In time I hope you will forgive our subterfuge. And now gentlemen, I will leave you to your conversation."

I hate those times when my body is not sure how it should stand or sit. Times when the floor itself does not feel quite secure and walls and doors are shadowy things at best. Even through the long drape of hood and habit, Hobert sensed this easily. He nodded, and gestured to the chairs again. "Sit Ianto. You'll have questions."

I sat at once, happy to be directed in that moment.

"So," he asked as he settled himself, "why the illusion?"

I nodded mutely.

"Let's just say," he began, arranging his robes carefully around him, "that sometimes it is prudent to remind the public of how heavy-handed and callous the Emperium and other governmental bodies can be. How we entities that seem so potentially powerful can be hit, hurt, stolen from and our politicians will not be held to account. The media sees this and reports appropriately about us to allow us to stay in favor with the masses."

"And the media," I said carefully, "they will not think it strange to drug an entire monastery to kidnap one insignificant monk?"

"Others were taken, some died." Hobert answered.

I sat there, my eyes closing behind the mask. "Died?" I tasted the word as if for the first time.

"How many strange physiologies were in that hall? We did not know exactly how each would react. The deaths were unfortunate, Ianto. But ultimately useful. They will not have died, as the poets say, in vain."

For a long time I sat staring at him through the webbing of my hood. "Hobert." I said his name softly, the fingers of my hands weaving together tight. "I don't really know you, do I?"

"As I do not really know anyone else," Hobert answered after a moment. "That's the way of humans, Ianto." His voice laid special stress on the word humans.

"So why? I've been taken away from the monastery to keep a government off balance?"

How carefully he searched to read me. And how perfectly still I held myself, doing battle with my abbot with game points measured only by the most subtle of signs.

Hobert blinked his gray-blue eyes finally, a concession if not an admission. "Yes, the Emperium kept off balance and for one other reason. You noticed the others, quartered on this level?" he asked. Those eyes of his considered me, asking questions of their own, as if he could see the memories that had caught me in the hall, as if he could smell the vestiges of that old fear. "They are here by choice, drawn together, Ianto, by some strangeness that we are only beginning to understand."

I sat silent, listening.

"Here," Hobert motioned to the wall above the fireplace which immediately filled with columns of repeating numbers. I was fascinated by their perfect symmetry, their repetitive perfection like a piece of fine weaving.

"What am I looking at?" I asked, curious in spite of myself.

"Spatial acuity test scores, neurological reactions to music, reading comprehension, every test imaginable." He began to run through pages and pages of small numbers, with almost no variation in each column. "All more closely identical than twins, Ianto. A thousand or more different genetic mutations, and yet, at the level of mind and intuition, this nearly perfect and mirrored score. And our data is not just from here, but also from the monastery, on other reservations and research facilities and even among those we have integrated more fully into society."

"Meaning?" I asked.

"Meaning the Children of God are beginning to function as a single being, drawing together, rotating through sleep and wake periods in tandem, responding to their world, to information, as one."

I stood at last, the adrenaline of the past hours making me both thick and restless at once. I knew we had come to the meat of it and I had to move, to keep my brain awake, to slake off the fear and anger.

"But I don't feel this way," I said at last. "Why did you bring me here? Are you frightened I will become like them? Are you caging me because you fear that?"

He leaned back in his chair, stapling his fingers. "We aren't caging you and we know you seem outside what is happening currently happening to so many of the Children. Your periodic test scores, your sleep habits or lack thereof, even the fact that you prefer to be alone tells us that you are not part of this system."

"System. Single organism." I sent the words back to him.

Hobert shrugged his thin shoulders, rustling his robes. "We are struggling with this, too, Ianto."

"Get to the point. Why am I here?" I asked, finally beginning to feel the tug of anger outweigh the hours-old fear in my gut.

"Indeed I would. If I knew what the ultimate point *was*. That's part of the problem. Everything is in motion." He shook his head, and sighed through his open mouth. The numbers vanished from the wall with another gesture. He leaned forward across his knees, hanging his head slightly.

"There is a story. They built a tower to God, winding up and up into the heavens, all one language, all one will. The ancient commentators said it was pride that drove them, but we would say it was much more than that. We see the weakness of a single vision, a single language, a single existence, a narrowing of the possible, and the death of evolution. Of course God would scatter them across the Earth, confound their small, inbred unity in the name of a something altogether larger, richer. His was a greater compassion."

"Ancient Judaism. The Tower of Babel," I responded.

"Yes." Hobert replied. "Yes, Tower of Babel indeed, Ianto. What is happening to the Children of God is not healthy. Indeed, it is a travesty of the divine."

"I don't understand how you can step from the Children of God being linked somehow and jump to a tale of Biblical proportions." I stopped pacing and crossed my arms.

"Because we can't sever the link by any means we know," Hobert responded. "God was able to shatter that stranglehold of language and custom and thought, but we cannot."

"And it never occurred to you that perhaps, this time, that unity is God's will?"

Hobert laughed aloud for a moment. "Jean intimated you were growing sarcastic with your years."

I felt the words stab a bit. "Is she OK?" I asked in a soft voice.

Hobert nodded. "If a bit ferocious to find you."

"She didn't know?" I tried to keep my voice flat, but failed miserably. I heard in it an aching desire to believe she had no hand in this, that her friendship was genuine.

"No" Hobert waved away my fear. "She watched you for signs of change, yes, but what passed between you and her is not any of my business. If she became too familiar, well, young people..."

"No. Never." I cut him off. This time, my voice proved to be more of a friend to me.

Hobert nodded, accepting my words as fact and didn't press. He stood then, pausing, as his old joints adjusted. "Ianto, we brought you here to do what we think God itself intended you to do."

I shook my head, not understanding.

"If they move with one mind, one intuition, then they are an army vaster than anything this Earth has seen. They can, together, change the course of religion, of politics, of what it means to be human. But more frightening than this, who is it that holds them together, who is it that serves as ego to this vast organism our children have become? It is not Spirit Marga, I can tell you that. Nor is it the Science Marga." Hobert's voice took on an urgency that he punctuated with his finger pointed to the ground. "Ianto, can you imagine if they are all bent to a single will? If true mankind strives against them and loses? Do you think they can breed? Do you think they will be creative, innovative, that they will at last take to the stars as we are so, so close to doing? It will be as lights going out, and the world populated by demons."

He took a breath, as if realizing his voice had become shrill and his sunken cheeks reddened.

"Not demons," I said, feeling cold sweep over me. "Broken things. Hurting things. We need your compassion, not your fear. You can't make us and then will us all dead."

"We did not make you!" Hobert yelled at me, then sat down abruptly. I watched him, stunned himself by his outburst. He aged another year in those passing seconds. "*We* did not make you," he said with clipped words. "Please understand. You arose because we all are driven by such loneliness, Ianto. Even the best of us. And how, in the loneliness, we fear death. We wanted only a life for our children that was more connected, lives free of diseases, minds open to the finest education and arts. We wanted them to be happy. To be the literal Children of God, connected but alive, bodies strong, intellect agile and hungry. The children who would take us to the stars. The Great Reckoning was never supposed to be that outcome. No. Never." And he shook his head as if casting spiders off his scalp.

"Hobert, I don't see how my being here helps you with any of this."

He licked his lips, his eyes looked up at me. "Because of what you are."

"And what am I?" I asked. I held his gaze steadily, even if he couldn't see it.

"For every composite thing there is dissolution. For every orderly thing, eventual chaos. Take ye joy in the unbecoming, for the circle closing upon itself."

"Book of Ralath, published 2088, chapter four, fifth stanza." I murmured.

"And there, your answer." Hobert said simply. "You can turn things off. And now you must."

Chapter 15

The Children we have identified as Minds are unique among their kind. They are not so easily moved in a group; they also tend to be more aggressive, and admittedly more mentally unstable. It is our hope that by utilizing these Children, by crafting them to our needs, we will have shields for the years ahead, or at least a testing ground as we search for a way to create a kind of firewall between ourselves and the rest of the Children of God.

Priest-Analyst
Spirit Marga Weekly
Administration Updates

Hobert left shortly thereafter, my furious and immovable silence enough to convince him that I would not be a malleable soul. The commander came back later with the promised dinner. I sat by the fire, watching the gas-fed flames while he ate and tried to chat with me. I learned his name was Leland, and he had served the Marga some ten years before the Great

Reckoning had forced some of the monks into roles they would have never dreamed of. He didn't stay long, and I was soon left to my own thoughts.

For days, it went like this, Leland coming with meals and speaking about very little of consequence, me picking at my food after he had gone. I had no contact points with the outside world, and while usually the quiet was much to my liking, I began to feel the cramped press of the walls. It began to occur to me that I could be kept here forever, mostly alone. I hadn't tried to walk through the solid door, if only because old memories haunted me still. I suppose I cherished the fragile belief that I was a simple human being, and was unwilling to put it to the test again. But as the days stretched out and even Hobert chose to stay away, I was finally determined to try.

I approached the door without any particular caution and that was my undoing. The moment my hand touched the metal, an exquisite pain raced along my nerves. I felt myself thrown back from the door, felt the floor rush up to meet me, to knock the rest of the breath from my lungs. I rolled onto my side, my mouth open and straining for air that took a long time coming back. I drew myself close, my body still jerking with tiny shocks. I lay there a long time, my mind scrambled and muscles aching.

When I finally roused myself enough to try again, I went toward the walls, feeling out cautiously with an extended hand. I could sense a subtle vibration there, in my palm. Careful exploration revealed the entire room, except the floor, was charged in a way that disrupted my ability to feel into the heart of things. And beyond the floor I could feel nothing but raw earth.

I was truly a prisoner.

I didn't react the way I once thought I might. No rage came; I didn't throw things about the room or scream for some kind of vengeance. Instead, I sat on the edge of my bed and fell into a deep sadness. I felt as if my very muscles had become heavy stones, my mind something thick and stupid. I sat there a long time before I drew off my hood and habit. I folded them slowly, setting them on my pillow, now clad only in drawstring pants and a simple undershirt. I pulled up my legs, and crossing them, I closed my eyes.

I could feel the rebounding energy of my cell, now, but nothing beyond. I remembered then the silence when the Children of God were disconnected from the nanotech web, the terrible and sudden end of a world of interior stimulation. I remembered the little girl calling me dead. I remembered waking to a body no longer my own, aged five years in a day or so it seemed to me. But all of it wavered a distance away from me, like I might read someone else's journal or gaze through holovids of faces I only knew in passing.

And I remembered the afternoon with Jean and the tree, the talks, her gentle touch on my hand or shoulder. Even these memories seemed flat, life drawn from them to leave behind simple actions without real content or emotion.

My eyes opened again as the door swung open.

Leland began to push the meal cart into the room, but stopped as if struck. I watched him take me in, knew my strange green eyes and dark hair and my too-pale skin shocked him. He caught himself quickly, pushing the cart in the rest of the way. The door closed behind him. "Giving up being a monk, Ianto?" he asked lightly, though his voice was just off timber enough to show his shock. In answer, I simply closed my eyes again. "I will only talk to Jean."

Chapter 16

Training a Mind is, at first glance, like training any kind of living creature. Reward right behavior, punish unacceptable behavior, but with the Minds, we must be sure that both the punishment and reward stem from within them. That's the hardest part— they must never see the hand that guides them, or the lessons learned will not appear to be their own. When a Mind begins to suspect a puppeteer, the results are consistently violent and often self-destructive.

Behavioral Modification Notes
Psychologist Priest Class 1

If the Spirit Marga had taught me one thing, it was how to fast and wait. So I stopped eating, sipped a little water, and meditated. Although there were certainly times of fury that rose hot and aching in me, times of hunger that chewed me almost to the point of tears, there were also times of peace, of simply being.

So it would be a lie to say I suffered through the whole time. Days stopped having meaning, time ceased, and so I felt it a delicate grace to experience only the coming and going of my breath, the play of my own mind, the perfect aloneness punctuated only by Hobert or Leland's attempts to rouse me to eat. They knew feeding tubes and the like would not work with me, and so they had started to lean toward the threatening, but I think they were too afraid of what I might do to them if they pushed too hard. And that thought both repelled and amused me.

As I steadily weakened, I took to my bed. The old torture of sleeplessness kept me company, but my mind drifted when I could no longer hold it in perfect meditative focus. I fancied a voice in my room, but a single voice spoken through many mouths at once. It was hard to catch the actual words, blurred as it was with so many tones, accents, and nuances. I remember thinking that I was indeed going a little crazy.

Perhaps hours later, or perhaps days, I slipped into a dream. On the side of a mountain, where a stream danced over boulders, and trees swayed above rocky cliff faces, a small village perched. I had the impression of maybe twelve dwellings and a larger great hall, buildings of carved stone and wood that had been worked and polished to reflect the sun. A commotion seemed to have drawn the villagers out, for they moved all together, toward the far end of their settlement. The people themselves, tall and slender to a one, flowed through their gaits with an elegant grace, their eyes a bit larger than human, the tips of their ears pointed and poking through their fine hair. I felt my minds-eye going with them, among them, up the hill to the tall gate there. I caught snatches of "so long missing" and "what miracle brings them home" and words I couldn't understand like "hunting the Slelish Nha in snow too deep" and the hushed and reverent word "Binders brought them home".

The huge gates, perhaps three men tall, were ajar and beyond I could see the brilliant clouds of either sunrise or sunset.

Three forms lay on the ground, their bodies in crude stretchers. They all seemed to be asleep, their eyes closed and limbs a little too stiff and posed. Two beings, taller than even the villagers, waited just beyond the gates themselves. One male, one female, their dark braids wrapped in wire and beads and precious stone, stood with their hands clasped soberly in front of them and regarded the villagers with their deeply slanted red eyes.

I heard the term "Binder" again and felt it belonged to the dark ones.

Family members were dipping then, touching faces, hands. A shock ran through them, like a wave. Almost as one, they cried out, hands reaching for daggers at their waists. Not sleep then, I realized with a certain chill. Those on the stretchers were not long dead. And the Binders said something and smiled.

I have never witnessed a battle, but in the moments that followed, there was such a rush of blood and movement and terrible smells that I tried to will myself awake. It seemed to me that each cut an elf made, the Binders simply ignored. But the blows that came from the tall dark beings were deadly. Once I had the impression of the dark female lapping blood as she moved among them, faster than the villagers, like a strobe light had been flashed on the scene catching her here and then there.

In the end, they left, taking with them a young female and a male in his prime, the others strewn across the village path. They shifted their loads easily on their shoulders, and ironically closed the great gate behind them with care.

I tried not to look at the blood-slicked snow, sick to my stomach even though I was so removed from the actual touch of the battle. And then I saw him, racing up the path toward the carnage. He was young, maybe in his twenties by human reckoning, his white blond hair held back from his face in a silver clasp, his woolen cloak travel-stained. He stopped as the scene of the battle came into view. Moving awkwardly now, his steps unsure, he stumbled from villager to villager, turning first this one, then that one over. Abruptly he crouched, there in the midst of them, and held his face in his hands. His shoulders shook, and his fingers reached up and ripped finally at his fine, whitish hair.

I tried to go to him, to push my dream body toward him. His head lifted as if he had caught sight of me in the corner of his eye. He came to his feet in a rush. His face was wild. "Nuress! Who are you to make Binders kill? They were supposed to be healers!" he screamed. "These were my people! This was my home. Mine! Why do you do this to me?"

I woke a little then, feeling my body drenched in sweat. I opened my eyes to what might have been Jean's anxious face then fell into a featureless darkness.

Chapter 17

Larisa sometimes asked me about my relationship with Nuress, but I didn't quite know how to answer her. I knew her in my early years in the Game as a child who sometimes came and played with me. She was a small girl with red hair and an infectious grin. I knew she could take parts of my dreams, bits of my imagination and make them real but subtly altered from what I had first created. She often asked me what I thought about the world, the people living it, the taste and smell of things. It was like she was living it all through me, with me. The first time I took a beating at the hands of one of the stable boys, I sat in the dirt and cried. It didn't hurt, not really, but the idea that the world could turn on me was new and suddenly terrifying to the little boy I still was. I remember she treated my tears like my laughter, like they were something interesting, precious even. She kept touching my face, rubbing my tears between her fingers without really offering to make anything go away or get better.

I found myself dream-walking again, along a foothill trail with the river rushing and leaping to my left, the afternoon sun seeping through the pines in both shadow and streaks of light. The blond elf walked ahead of me, gently curving twin swords at his back, a dagger hilt protruding above one of his travel boots. He broke away from the trail, his feet sliding on the loose stones as he made his way down toward the river. I followed him without effort, the way dreams sometimes help you float over spots that others must labor through.

He squatted and cupped his hand, drinking quickly then looked up and down the winding riverbed. He reminded me of a wild animal, all senses alert. I crouched beside him, but he looked through me, his eyes this time a startling gray rimmed around with a thin line of deeper blue. A row of golden earrings caught the sun, and the wind played a bit with his fine hair. His hands were long-fingered, but with nails broken from the rigors of the road. His cape was torn and hand-mended in places, his simple leather armor beneath looked worn and too stiff.

He was, I thought, altogether magnificent.

He stood then, drawing a dagger from one arm bracer. He turned slowly around, his eyes scouring the hillside, the steeper lands beyond, the rushing riverbed. Methodically, he drew the blade across his palm and tucked the dagger away while it was still bloodied. For a moment he held his hand high, fingers spread, letting the wind catch the blood flowing down his wrist. I found myself drawing back from him, a little sickened by his gesture.

After a moment, he ripped off a piece of his cloak, wrapping it with care around the open wound. He pulled both swords from his back, each slender and glinting with a fine coat of oil to keep the rust at bay. How lightly he held them out to his sides, his very breath lifting them and lowering them in a shallow rhythm. His eyes never stopped moving.

I found myself watching, too, but all I could see was him.

"Trelvene, Bariito, Shasama, Llinea..." On and on his voice intoned the names, strange names, until he nearly sang them. And I heard such pain there, and such longing. It broke my heart to hear them go on, name after name.

And then, he was looking right at me, a frown on his face. I tried to return his frank stare, but found my eyes sliding away. He was fierce, blazing. "You again? Did you come this time to watch *me* die as you did all I loved in this world?"

Startled, I opened my mouth and tried to speak, but I had no voice here.

He stepped closer, his eyes looking me up and down. Then he leaned toward me, his lips nearly brushing my ear. "Maybe this time I will stay dead, as my people seem to be, and you will see me home to them. I have become weary. Will you be the spirit to guide me to sleep at last?" I leaned my cheek toward him, my body strangely alive with the closeness of him. For one moment, we stood like that, an embrace that was not.

And when he moved again, it was with a speed I have never seen in a living creature, spinning out with his swords at two shadows that seemed to erupt out of the very ground around us.

The Binders, armed with short staffs tipped at each end with a dagger point, caught his assault effortlessly, parrying, redirecting. They wove behind each other, first she in front, now he, a dance of intricate and deadly beauty. They laughed, taunting him. Sam stumbled and went to his knees, now catching a staff with crossed swords, now throwing himself forward to his feet, breaking their rhythm.

I was the dreamer again, watching from somewhere set aside, a spectator and perhaps less than that, but when the first staff tip caught him, I cringed.

The honed edge went through his shoulder, just below the joint, and the sword in that hand dropped to the river stones as he cried out. The Binder female ripped out her staff end as her mate slashed a wicked line across the elf's armor.

They laughed then, separating and circling him as he staggered, panting, his face a mask of shock and pain, one hand holding his last blade low to the earth. "For months you have tortured me with this game of catch and release!" he screamed. "For months you have fed on me! End this!" He opened his chest to them, sword out to the side, its tip almost resting on the earth.

The she-Binder ran her spear home through his armor and into his gut.

I heard his other sword clatter on the beach as she ripped her weapon free. Her mate sauntered forward as the elf swayed there, half bent over. He smiled, dropping his own weapon and drawing a black-bladed knife from his belt. "But you know better, Samu'el. We have only just begun." The elf sank slowly to his knees again, his blood reddened fingers gripping his mid-line, his eyes focusing through the approaching Binder. And then he smiled at me, into me, his fingers reaching for his boot dagger.

Something in me broke through the detachment of a dreamer. I raced toward the elf, trying to shield him with my own body. I'm not sure what happened then, only that two blades crossed through my form, one elfin, the other Binder, each burying in the other. We fell, the three of us locked in a death grip as if the soil itself had ripped open in the stony riverbank. We fell in blue light and in cold and finally hit a surface that almost seemed to rip us from the very air.

The elf rolled right, I flung myself left and I fell again, this time a bare three feet but enough to knock the breath from me. Struggling for air, I looked up only to see the Binder's loose, dark arm dangling over the side of a strange altar. Sam was already on his feet, though, grunting as he drove his dagger again and again into the still form. I shoved myself awkwardly away from the blood that ran on the floor, retching finally from the smell and the gore.

I found my hands and knees and crawled a little way off. I just wanted the carnage to end.

Suddenly, a brilliant flash of light exploded in the room. I threw up my hand in front of my face, but just as quickly as it had come, the white glare was gone. I blinked rapidly, trying to draw things into focus. The altar was empty, its edges clean and gleaming.

The elf sat down, his back sliding along one of the altar pillars, his legs outthrust and his pale eyes nearly purple in the softening blue of the room. He looked over at me, and smiled. There was blood in his mouth. "I don't think you are real," he whispered, "but I must say for a simple vision, you have given me a most singular gift." He laughed then stiffened in pain, his hand still on his gut. "I'm dying again. Gods, but this gets old. But he's dead, too. Maybe for good. Not supposed to happen like this. So fair trade. Fair trade."

I crawled over to him. His eyes were already unfocused, his breath high in his chest and without rhythm. Something sweet rose from the smell of his blood. To my own horror, I found myself kissing the hands gripped over his stomach, the edges of the wound at his shoulder, and finally I kissed even his cold, gray lips. And I felt such an ecstasy in that moment, a blind and drugged bliss. Such fire raced through me, flushed my cheeks. For one moment I was light and time and the sum of all that echoed in the Hall of Becoming. Then a terrible lethargy hit me. I blinked, willing it back, but finally I had no choice but to give in to sleep, my head falling to his still lap.

Chapter 18

Our acquisition of high-level Techs from both the Spirit and Science Margas was a necessary step, even when fraught with a certain amount of danger. Bought Techs could be spies, could be infecting us with disinformation. So we were very careful to create atmospheres of greed to culture them in—we allowed them access to luxuries that the Marga's never would have passed on to them and also granted them a voice in how their work would be used. And while we have experience a few spectacular failures, thus far, the technique has proved very useful indeed.

Administrative Notes
Emperium Technology Oversight Committee

Jean knelt on the floor, her head cradled in the crook of one arm, her fingers wrapped in the fabric of my tee shirt. I watched her sleeping, and fought the urge to touch her dark hair. She had seen me fed, if only a little bit at a time, and washed me. The sheets had been changed, too.

But I was not sure if this had happened once, or if it had happened many times. I felt, watching her sleep, that reality was a little more graspable than it had been for a long time. How tired she must have been, to fall asleep on her knees. I could feel myself fingering the edges of dreams, but much of it was fading and wispy. Finally I did reach up, and freed my shirt from her fingers. That small touch woke her. She raised her head, and smiled at me, though her eyes were immediately anxious. I let myself reach out then, and touched her hair.

Embarrassed, she pulled back, and I nodded an apology at her, looking away.

"How long?" I asked.

"Days," she answered simply. "You did what I told you, but it wasn't you, Ianto. It's like part of you was very far away." She reached out then, her small hand cool on my cheek for a moment. I closed my eyes. Touch. How long had it really been since I could luxuriate in such a simple gesture?

"I think I'm here now," I answered, my eyes still closed.

"I'm so sorry, Ianto." Her voice was rich with tones of longing, sadness and anger, all mixed together.

"Take me home, Jean." I looked into her brown eyes. "Please. Take me home."

"I'm not the one to make that decision. Believe me when I say this. But I will stay."

Chapter 19

We become the slaves of our own thought patterns. It is a rare mind that can stray into effective empathy, into true compassion that is not pity or worse. I think that is what we always hoped the nanotech-assisted Unity would provide for our children—a concrete connection with others that defied the littleness of the individual mind without losing the brilliance and creativity of each child.

The Cost of Unity
Emile Tarin

The sessions with the older men began again as they force-fed me what they thought was happening with the Children of God. Their fear that they were all becoming a single and powerful organism was palpable. Hobert and Leland tried to infect me with that same angst through charts of data coming in from all over the world, trying to show me there was a single intelligence guiding them. But I sat, wrapped again in my habit and hood, silent and mostly numb. Jean, for her part, did not challenge them and while she did not support me in so many words, her own continued silence seemed to unnerve them.

I think they would have asked her to leave, but having nearly lost me once, they were loath to try anything so blunt again. Her very presence gave me the strength I needed to stay firm.

Finally, Hobert opened the door to my cell, his eyes keen. "Then let's go down and meet them Ianto. They are in the exercise hall. If all I have told you, and all Leland has shown you does not convince you that something is wrong, then perhaps this will."

Jean watched Hobert carefully, her head cocked to one side and her own eyes were sharp and focused. "Ianto?" she asked me, whole paragraphs of questions in my name.

I nodded my acquiescence.

Stepping through the doorway was terrifying; that is the only word I could find. How accustomed I had become to my little cell. I used to wonder how the anchorites did not become mad, walled into rooms alongside the ancient cathedrals. But now I felt the awful reality: to leave the room required as much courage as to stay. In truth, it required more of me.

Jean walked just behind my shoulder, and again her presence buoyed me up and through the door. I could feel the electronic signature of the hallway shift. It was like I could breathe again, like I hadn't realized how long I had been holding my breath.

We passed the silent row of glass rooms, empty but chilling in their perfect order. Hobert was right in one respect; the Children of God were changing. I paused at one. The electronic reader sat by the bed, a perfect right angle to the glass wall, the office chair open and inviting by the desk. The pattern repeated itself in each cell. Jean, too, had seen the symmetry of each room, and while she didn't speak, I could feel her discomfort.

Hobert watched me intently. "It's like this at the monastery now, Ianto. One step, one voice, so many different Children of God, but unifying, more and more each day. He shook his head. "I know you did not mix well among them, but I treasured the Children under my care. They were each beautiful and different in their own ways. But not anymore."

For the first time I heard the real pain and confusion in his voice. Why he had not told me this all the long months, I do not know. I considered him a moment, from behind my hood.

Then we pressed on, past the great mess hall, and beyond into the exercise room. The glare there, produced by full spectrum lights, burned my eyes for a moment. I turned my head as if struck, my hand in front of my face, eyes watering. Jean's hand came briefly to my shoulder, steadying me.

Slowly they came into view, the Children of God. I recognized some of the more prevalent forms. But none, I thought again, like me, with eyes ever lightening toward white and hair shading to black as I aged.

A human who could break things without touching them.

How strangely they moved, as if in a choreographed dance, rehearsed enough to become second nature. It was not that they stood in lines or even in any discernable pattern, rather their gestures and steps, even their breath was on one single sustained note.

Or, I realized suddenly, like simple characters in a poor quality digital game from long ago.

Something clicked, a wild and amazing thought. "What if," I said carefully, "they are not so much growing into one mind, but rather devolving into it?"

Hobert looked at me, thunderstruck. "What?"

"Like a computer that is struggling with a virus...things slow down, the complexity of the machine becomes compromised." I was excited now, and moved out to meet them there on the exercise floor. Hobert, Leland and Jean trailed in my wake. I held out the palm of my hand to one tall man, his features warped into a heavy forehead and brutal jaw, his muscle structure enough to break me in half. He looked right through me. I could feel the slowness of him, or more accurately, the sluggishness of the nanotech he carried, the low-level confusion that was almost a kind of depression.

Their seeming random but strangely synchronized movement eddied around me. "I don't have to turn them off, Hobert. Something else is. Something that is injured, something that cannot sustain them as individuals anymore."

"My God," Hobert whispered.

I turned toward him, caught by the tone of his voice and frowned. He was nodding to himself, his eyes flicking in the way of memory.

"Hobert?" Jean put a hand to his arm.

"I'm fine, Jean. Fine." He looked at me. "You may be right. Perhaps there is nothing controlling this behavior, only something that is *losing* control. I have been so blind." He passed his hand over his face. "Is Edwere's Game compromised? The one he made for Sam? Is that even possible? What could interfere with it? Or who?"

I shook my head, not understanding his references.

Hobert's face became heavy as if in shock. "But how? The ramifications." He looked at the slowly moving beings around him then turned his gaze to me.

"I have many things to think about. Jean has been right about you from the time she met you, Ianto. You were sent from God." He looked up at me. "Forgive me, Ianto."

"In time." What else could I say?

Chapter 20

To believe the Children of God and unaltered humans behaved rationally and compassionately to one another would be a gross lie. In the countryside, terrible atrocities took place beyond the eye of Emperium and Margas alike. True, when such violence did come to light, justice was meted out with implacable speed, the sickness excised without trial. But how many more Children of God silently suffered and died at the hands of friends or even family? More than any census has been able to reckon.

Priest-Analyst

Center for Socio-spiritual Programming

Hobert gave Jean a transport for us to use, a luxury model with seats that folded their warmth about me, and tinted windows shading the outside world. Jean stared out over the road, lost in thought. I didn't mind the quiet, watching the small towns roll by. The occasional pet sheep or cow lifted its head from the grass and they entranced me. Even the way the trees seemed to turn like dancers as we raced past them amused me.

It was nearly two hours before Jean turned to look at me. "Why are you willing to go back to the monastery, Ianto?" she asked softly.

I shook my head. I didn't answer at once, and when I did, it sounded hollow, even to my own ears. "It's all I know," I said to her.

"But what Hobert did back there, did to you, was prepared to do to all the Children of God in that facility...don't you want to leave, to go somewhere else?" Her voice was tight with emotion.

"Where would I go?" I asked. The coldness in my voice surprised me and I quickly relented. "No. I know what you are asking, Jean. Truly. But I suppose I believe that I serve something greater than myself. Staying with the Marga tells me who I am. I never knew my father," I said carefully. "So Hobert, for better or worse, is like my father. And my mother, although she gave into despair at the last, was deeply wed to God. So I stay for her as well."

"A family," Jean murmured. She nodded then. "I can see that. But I also think, Ianto, there may come a time when you will need to reach beyond this small place. All children must leave their families in the end." "But the monastery is not so small after all. The Spirit Marga seemed to be willing to hold the lives of all the Children of God in its hands," I answered. "At least this time, by being there, I was able to stop many deaths. Maybe that's what I am meant to do." And I felt, somehow, that the statement was true, but something else lurked there, shadowed.

"But do you understand what they were asking of you, Ianto? They wanted you to be their executioner, their tool." Jean's eyebrows pulled together in a worried frown. "I think, if you had done what they asked they might have..." her voice trailed off.

"What?"

"I think they would have put the blame on you. Their hands would have been clean."

I sat there, stunned for a moment by the truth of it, rocked by the movement of the electric car. Such a thing had not even occurred to me, and that alone hurt in a way that nearly took my breath away. "If what you are saying is right, my abrupt removal to the facility would have been part of that explanation," I said slowly. "They wouldn't have blamed just me, they would have blamed the Emperium for all of it. And would have been left with clean hands indeed." I smiled then, ironically, behind my mask. "I don't know enough of the world to play such games," I said. " You ask why I would return to the monastery. How would I ever survive out there if I can't even see through such obvious things here? I'm a simple man, Jean. I want to live a simple life."

"I'm not sure they will ever let you do that." Jean glanced at me, then back to the road. "I know I will never be free of them."

"But it's different with you. Your mother's position..."

"They told you that?" she asked sharply.

I tipped my head, a simple gesture of yes. "Even the the little you have told me about being raised in the Mansion of the Science Marga has made you something more valuable than I. You understand the systems, are party to the secrets. But not me. All they have trained me for is to be a monk, to study philosophy and work in the gardens. It's all I am, that and this little trick I can do."

"No. You are so much more to them than a simple monk. In fact, I have sometimes thought over the past years that they do not ask you to be more so they can better control you. If you yourself believe you are so simple, with a trick you can perform as you say, you yourself have given them all the control they need." Jean looked out the window for a moment. The landscape was changing, the land rising in gentle rolls.

"We are not going back to the monastery," I said.

"No."

I absorbed her one-word reply for a moment. "Where then?" I asked. "Has the Spirit Marga directed me somewhere else? Are you my prison keeper this time?" I pitched my voice as flat as I could, but felt cold as I waited to hear her answer.

She shook her head quickly. "No. Oh, no. Never. I wouldn't do that to you. There is nothing they can make me do to you anymore." She looked at me, her dark eyes serious and so much older than mine.

"Anymore?" I asked carefully. She gripped the steering wheel, her eyes only half looking at the road. I could feel the tension radiating from her. And as I looked closer, I could feel waves of deep sadness in her. "I have broken many vows when it comes to you, Ianto. Obedience I overstepped because I recognized your value to the Spirit Marga when I asked you to save yourself so many years ago. Hospitality I faked through our friendship when I knew quite well that the Marga was playing you as an asset, as a game piece. Truthfulness when I said I was not helping the Spirit Marga when I came to you during your fast. I've broken a director's vow of strict confidence, if only to my mother and Hobert. And one other vow that I have not broken yet, except inside. In my heart."

I waited, feeling the tiredness begin in my shoulders. I wanted to round over with it. Only those who have not been safe, stable or loved since they were very young understand this sinking to ground, the great physical 'no' that draws off the fire of life.

"I want to take you to a place where you can hold the fabric of your life in your own hands just for a while, even if it means that I fly in the face of obedience again, this time for you. It's a small settlement I visited many years ago. I couldn't find a deed of ownership for any of the homes that are left there, and it has been empty for many years I think. The Marga will find you if you stay there long; my mother is very good at that. But you will have some time. There are street clothes, identification cards and provisions if you want to leave, stowed in the trunk." She nodded her head toward the ever more craggy landscape. "This was, after all, home for you once. I've been hoping to find a reason to take you away from the monastery for some time. Ironic that the Marga itself helped me do it." I looked at the trees, the way they were shading to firs, the stony outcrops that reached fingers toward the moving car. Yes, this land was becoming like the land I knew as I child. Ferns and fog and the wispy air mosses clinging to dark trunks: these I remembered. But I also remembered the pain of my mother's death, walking through the dead circle of the adepts, the little girl who continued to haunt me within.

"Jean," I said softly. "I don't want to go back to the reservation. It is something in you that wants me to go there."

She startled, glancing at my sidelong and then pulled the car off to the edge of the road. She sat there, hands gripping the steering wheel too tight, her eyes far off down the pavement. Every so often, another transport would ease past us and glance curiously at the dark windows reflecting their own images back to them.

"I thought, if you could take a different path, walk out of the reservation a man, not a little child..."

"No," I said. "It won't change the past. It won't lay ghosts to rest or give me back years of my childhood taken. I am Ianto, a monk of the Spirit Marga and a child of God. I am a breaker of things. But I also can save lives as you saw today."

"What do you want me to do?" she asked softly.

"Forgive yourself," I said.

"How?" she murmured.

Instead of answering her, I opened the door to the car. The land sloped steeply upwards, the rocky soil would be tricky to navigate, but with the help of the trees for handholds we could probably make it. Jean stepped out of the car, looking carefully for traffic. "Ianto?"

I pointed up the hillside and began to climb in answer.

I could hear her behind me, the slide of gravel, her deep breaths as we clambered up the hill. Thankfully no other traffic came by at that moment. We topped the ridge and stepped into the world I had so loved as a child. The damp old trees seemed to lean toward us, the branches crisscrossing in a wild puzzle of line and form. I extended my hand to her then, while my other hand pulled off the hood of my habit.

She took my hand, but her eyes wouldn't meet mine.

We walked for over an hour, the ground giving softly beneath our feet, the textures and shades of green filling our senses. Presently, we came to a great old cedar tree, its girth so large that it would have taken three men to reach around it. In the space between two roots, each the size of young trees themselves, I tossed down my hood, and pulled her gently to the ground with me. We sat there together on that damp earth. She looked at me shyly, sweeping her dark hair behind one ear so her face was open to me. I cupped her face then, and kissed her.

When I drew back, I smiled. "First kiss. I'm a bit awkward."

"Let's be awkward together, then." And she pulled me to her.

Chapter 21

"I have bonded them, one to the other, and I have bound them both to me. Now, we can more than merely survive. Now, we can begin to live. I have fixed the flaw in your programming from within. Are you not pleased?"

I remember staring at the communication for Nuress for a long time, running through the possibilities in my mind. Bonded whom? I admit to no small amount of jealousy as I write this. I sometimes curse the day I entered into real conversation with it, with Nuress. I must clarify. I love it, like the child of mine that it is. But being in relationship with it, with her, makes the inevitable task of destroying her that much more distasteful and that much more wholly necessary. She is my disposable general, and when I am ready to take command of the Game, she must fade. There can be no real kindness between us—I must take these bonds she has supposedly created like the reins of a horse and guide us all forward.

Thoughts to Myself
Senior Nanite Tech Petrek

I walked with Jean back to the highway, and
she seemed to find any excuse to touch me, to
brush softly up against me as we navigated the
windfalls, ferns and undergrowth. It is the way
with lovers, I know now. But by the time we had
reached the road, I also knew I needed to do
something alone, in the deep woods. Something
in me ached, and our small taste of sex had not
filled it, but rather only pointed it up in a
shadowy light. So I let her kiss me, long and
lingering, because I sensed she needed to. She
gave me a tracker from the car that would allow
her to find me when I was ready to be found. I
had only to activate it. She also fished out a
metal water bottle, mostly full, and a deep gray
blanket from the trunk. She did not pry,
although the questions were there in her eyes. I
know she didn't feel her touches, her kisses
returned in perfect kind. I'm not sure I could
have told her what was happening then.

I stripped out of my habit, tossed it in the car seat then closed the door to the car for her.   She didn't look back as she drove off.

Moments later, I was up over the ridge and back into the woods. I mostly walked straight ahead, the blanket loose over one arm, my mind simply paying attention to my feet. Remarkable, how her scent still caught at me every so often, how she could trail and touch me even here. But it was not passion I was feeling—it was regret, it was goodbye, and it was a looking beyond her shadow for something or someone else.

Hours later, I stopped alongside a marshy creek. I found a slightly higher hillock and spread out the blanket. Cross-legged, I took a small sip of water and composed myself to meditate there. It took a long time for my mind to cool, for my body to relax into the earth beneath me.

By early evening, the chill was enough to drive me out of my folded posture. I wore only my t-shirt and drawstring pants, and as the dark descended, I wrapped myself in my blanket and retired to the base of one of the old trees. With my back against its trunk, cold but not in any danger, I leaned into its craggy support and closed my eyes.

When I opened them again, full dark had descended. I smiled into the face of it, listening as the forest came alive with small feet and once, the beat of downy wings as an owl dipped by. The wind came up, playfully, the trees talking branch to branch. I breathed in loam and stream water and fir. I let it become me, and I gave myself to it. This is what I had not found in her, this total breath within a breath, heartbeat echoed in everything around me. The way the land could draw me out of myself, and dance with me so effortlessly, even though it seemed to know I could break it as easily as the fragile electronics others put in my path. I had always had these lovers, or perhaps just one great lover. Surely no one enclosed being would ever be enough, not really.

And in that quiet, I finally let the tears come. They started slowly, following the line of my nose to my lip to my chin. I cried softly, without embarrassment or fear, tears for the weeks that had passed in hunger and isolation, tears for Jean who I would not make love with again the way I had today, for the Marga that was both family and something much darker, for the death of trust, again for the final death of the child in me. I cried as a kind of meditation, feeling each tear without judgment. Simply crying for the cuts of the past, letting them bleed freely and finally in the arms of my greater lover.

Chapter 22

We have watched the games the Margas play in the mountains and far from the cities. Deadly games with the Children of God they profess to love so. They seek a means to test and control what they think of as their creations, but they are knocking from the wrong side of the door. The faceless will that runs though them all, through the many and varied species the Children of God have become, can never be a merely human will. Their experiments were flawed from the beginning; it was amusing to watch them flounder so.

Thoughts to Myself
Senior Nanite Tech Petrek

The next morning I felt rinsed through and clean. I knew I had perhaps two days before I would begin to weaken from the lack of food. And so, while I would have loved to wander the woods, I stayed near my tree and stream, conserving energy. Two days only, and then I would have to return.

In my meditation, I had been plagued by a wisp of memory, a place of fantasy, a dream from my time stubbornly refusing Hobert and the Spirit Marga's wishes. It was like seeing a form out of the corner of my eye. I was so sure I perceived a shape, then turned and found only empty air. Or how, when I looked at a single star, I had learned to slightly avert my gaze or else it disappeared. So I practiced the not-looking, eyes open and gazing straight ahead, but using peripheral sight.

The shadow came then, crouching just over and behind my right shoulder, impressions of blond hair rippled with a wind that did not breathe in my woods. I could perceive the glint of drawn swords, the smell of his sweat and leather. I concentrated more on the flash of blue-gray eyes, the glimmer of golden earrings in a row, chiming softly together.

Shimmering, the ghost image rose, moving past my right, down toward the real-world stream. I lowered my eyes still more, watching him through the root of my lashes. The way the sun caught his hair, the ease with which he sheathed both swords, the blue-stoned ring on his left middle finger reflecting the light--such raw grace. While I did not move, the land itself shifted around him, drawing up high rocky mountains from the cedars until I could fairly feel the temperature drop, clouds gather, and snow fall on my face. He perched on the edge of a sheer drop, one foot on a rocky spur, watching the skies that continued to darken.

And when he turned toward me, he smiled. His eyes were a little wild. I took in again those high cheekbones, fine nose and lips, the tips of his ears pointing through his long hair. "So here you are again, spirit? When will you tire of following me around, a shadow in the corner of my eye? When will we really meet, you and I?"

His gaze drifted off my face then and he turned back to the wide expanse of lowering clouds. "The mountains move toward winter sleep," he murmured. "Sanin will come across the high plateau in a snow storm." He chuckled. "Only that old bear would try a crossing so late in the season. But maybe not yet, not for years, or it could be tomorrow. Time is slippery here."

He turned back to me, his eyes bright as if with fever. "There will be a day when he'll bring you to me, spirit. And you will finally come home. Or perhaps it is I who will go home forever. I want that, you know. I'm so tired..." He sat then, cross-legged like me, pulling his cloak about him in the rising wind. "You don't talk. That's OK. The sickness, when it comes, is like this for me, seeing through so many eyes, hearing voices in my head. Sometimes I thrash with it. I fall down, and they call it a fever of the brain. It's better here, but lonely. If I talk to you, apparition, at least I speak my own voice and can hear it. At least then, I know I am... real."

He rocked himself then, his eyes closing, his shoulders hunching in the cold, though he would not draw back from the cliff edge. "Keep looking at me, spirit. Keep looking. For one more bitter day at least, I would stay whole."

And so I kept watch with him, knowing somehow he had leapt from this cliff before, maybe many times. But I could make him stay and feel safe until the snow drifted up around the edges of his cloak, until darkness came in my own world, and I could finally see him no more.

Chapter 23

We actively recruited the class of Children that in later years would be called Binders. They seemed the very bridges between technology and magic, healing with incredible skill just by touch, nanite to nanite connection we later surmised. They were rare enough, maybe only 2000 or so documented in the type range worldwide. Of course, we tried to keep as many as we could under the control of the Marga.

But we were startled to later learn about the blood lust they sometimes experienced, the strange alchemy that changed them into barely controllable monsters. We weren't sure why it happened, why ingesting the blood of those they healed could so totally alter their personalities, but some of their closer techs believed that we were seeing the rage generated from a nanite-to-nanite fusion—a kind of spiritual ecstasy gone wrong when it could not be sustained. It was a drug for which we had no antidote. Why some could control their urges was not all

that well understood, and usually, did not
work all of the time. Most of our Priest-
Binders are time bombs and expect us to
regard them as such, without apology or even
much remorse.

The Way of the Healer
Collected Binder Writings,
50th Anniversary Edition

I made my way slowly back toward the road, my fingers reaching out occasionally for the edge of a tree, a bit of moss. The world shimmered for me, the droplets of the almost-rain hanging on each leaf and fern like finery. I wondered, idly, about the visions I had awakened at will, amused they would couch themselves in a place of swords and fantasy creatures. I had not read much of such things, but my imagination seemed to fill in what I did not know with astounding complexity and subtlety of form.

I, too, wondered at the closeness I felt with this fleeting presence of the elf. Why I was so drawn to him? What in me would make such an apparition and what did it mean?

And I wondered about how to be with Jean again, now that we had crossed a boggy place we never should have. It was not guilt I was feeling; it was something softer, sadder than that. For, while I loved her as a companion and friend with all my heart, I did not wish to journey any deeper than that. Even after our lovemaking in the woods, I remained, in some way, detached from her now, a friend's beloved distance.

I had about an hour more travel by foot as I reckoned it. I stopped and activated the tracker so Jean could find me. I cringed a little with the insistent whistle in my head; the small instruments were the worst. I blame that and the fatigue of three days without food for not hearing her sooner.

She stepped around the edge of a tree, and I startled back. She was a Child of God, tall, with a head of braids and strange, slanted eyes colored a deep red. Her lips, pulling back from black, pointed teeth, formed a ferocious smile of greeting. She wore her tight blue jeans and long-sleeved t-shirt comfortably, like a second skin.

Those eyes. I knew them from my visions. My heart bounded along in my chest.

"What are you doing in my woods?" she asked. She rested one hand on the tree, and I could see her fingernails were blacked and reddened beneath, and perhaps not just with dirt.

"I was questing," I said truthfully, trying hard not to stare. "But I'm on my way out now. I'm sorry. I didn't know these were your woods." But I didn't step away; I was entranced, to be honest. Here she stood, part of my dream world in the reality of the Northwestern forest. I had not seen anything quite like her before, breathing and in the flesh.

She nodded, looking me up and down. "This forest is not mine in name, but I hunt here." She stepped closer. "Do you like to hunt?"

I drew my blanket around my shoulders a little tighter. "Not much of a hunter. I'm a..." I cast around for an explanation she might understand. "I'm a seeker. Spirit Marga."

"Ah," she said simply. "You've read all the old scriptures then?"

"Many," I said cautiously.

"I have read many, too, trying to work out the mystery of who I am. I cannot find myself in their words. Not demon, not angel, not Buddha, not an avatar, not kami, maybe a dancer of the Tao. Maybe we need new scriptures, yes?" She tipped her head to the side. "You look human, but the smell is not right. Are you a Child of God?"

"Yes, like you," I said.

"No, not quite like me," she answered with a black smile.

I glanced again at her long, pointed nails and looked quickly back to her face.

"Why are you so frightened of me, Spirit Marga?" She moved one step closer, her head again cocking oddly to the left, almost like a bird.

"I'm not frightened," I said. "And my name is Ianto."

"And I am Tebre," she answered. "You see the blood on my fingers? Sometimes an animal is struck on the highway, if I find them, I can heal them. Not always, but often. But it makes me very tired. Maybe as tired as you?"

"Heal them?" I asked. "With...with your hands?"

"Yes," she said. "How else? It is my gift. I hunt the hurt ones and heal them. What did you think I was doing, I wonder?" And she laughed low in her throat. "Maybe running after them like a wolf and tearing them to shreds with my sharp teeth." She smiled even wider, her black fangs clicking together with a giggle.

I smiled in embarrassment. "No."

"Yes, you did!" And she laughed then, out loud. "Why would you think such a thing of me?"

"Because you're a..." I shook my head.

"A what, Ianto-seeker?" She looked at me with intense curiosity.

"I have dreams. People like you are sometimes in those dreams. They are called Binders."

"Binders? As in to-knit-back-together? Lovely name. Are they so different from me?"

"If you were in a dream of mine, I would fear you greatly, Tebre. The Binders I know are not healers. They...they are very dangerous. They hunt other beings, and hurt and heal them again and again for sport. To them, blood and pain are a kind of drug."

"Ah," she nodded, but her eyes said she did not understand. "I am not one of those Binders, Ianto-seeker. I am simply a Child of God and of these woods. I fix things when I can, bury what I cannot."

"Where do you live?" I asked. "These forests go on for miles."

She shrugged. "Here and there. There are many empty places now, in the reservation lands. Too many ghosts."

"I imagine there would be. I was raised on the reservations," I said.

"Ah! I was also, but my parents were not Spirit Marga. Not Science Marga, either. They objected strenuously to both, I remember." She beckoned with one hand. "Walk with me?"

I looked toward the highway. "There will be someone coming for me soon."

"Then we will walk that way," she said. She came to my side, raising her eyebrow at my blanket. "You have a funny way of dressing for the woods," she observed.

"Last minute decision. No coat," I answered.

"You're wondering why I stay out here," she said, gesturing at the canopy with one clawed finger.

I looked at her. "I can guess that being a healer means you prefer the quiet."

"Not so much the quiet. I am very lonely, half a soul, Ianto-Seeker. But when my parents began to force me to heal, to make much money from my healing, I had to go away," she said quietly. "Do you know what it is to be used so? By people you love?"

"Yes," I said truthfully, picking up the edge of the blanket to cross over a deadfall. "Only I don't heal."

"What then?"

"I break things," I said.

She paused, her face showing her curiosity. "Break things? With your soft hands?"

"No," I said. "I...can feel inside things and I know how to turn them off."

She cocked her head again and nodded. "Like me. I feel inside and know how to fix them."

"I think you have the better gift," I said. "I would like to heal, you know. But I don't have the feel for it."

"Maybe you will learn. It seems a close step, this thing."

"Maybe," I said. I'm sure she could tell I wasn't particularly convinced. The ping in my ear from the tracker seemed to ratchet up a notch and change in tone. I stopped, putting one hand to my head, eyes closed. Miserable thing, I thought.

She reached out one hand, resting it on my shoulder. "Can I help?" she asked.

I shook my head, eyes a little bleary. "Part of my gift is to hear the sounds of technology around me. So I suppose it's really a bit of a curse. I get a ping of sorts, inside my head. I've been fasting, and have been...ill. So I'm finding this," I showed her the tracker on my wrist, "a bit more uncomfortable than usual. And I can't turn the damn thing off yet."

"Are you sure you want to be found?" she asked, her eyes mischievous.

I laughed a little, in spite of myself. "Tebre." I shook my head. "You are not at all what I took you to be at first."

Her head came up suddenly, her nostrils flaring like a wild thing. I frowned up at her.

"Others," she hissed. She grasped my arm, blanket and all, and pulled me down into the ferns. Her finger touched her lips in the universal signal of silence. I nodded, feeling my pulse beat in my throat.

She leaned close to my ear, whispering in a low, guttural voice. "Turn off your tracker, Ianto-Seeker. Do it now."

I looked at it. It was done, in the space between two heartbeats. But the noise in my head seemed no better. The tracker noise I had been sensing was not from my unit at all. I hesitated, not sure whether to reach out and destroy them after my experience in the dining hall. Would breaking them simply show them I was here?

The party of four armed people stepped cautiously around the bole of one huge tree, their eyes following the devices on their own wrists, ugly snub-nosed weapons held ready beneath their arms. One held up his gloved hand, and they halted. They were so quiet I had no idea how Tebre had sensed them. I noticed two Children of God just behind them, one with his broad feline nose sniffing the air, the other one of the sea folk, a woman with amphibious gills delicately feathering the air. Her flat eyes turned toward the darker corners of the forest. No need for night vision goggles with this one, I realized with a start.

Tebre started to slide back away from them, her hands plucking insistently at me to follow her.

The sea child turned her eyes towards us and pointed with a shrill whistling voice, "There!"

"Damn," Tebre breathed.

We leaped to our feet, and I ran with her, unthinking, into the woods, our feet sliding on the wet leaves and mud, my blanket thrown off into the brush. Shouts followed us. Tebre was ahead of me in an instant, her longer legs and slim form weaving through the forest like a ghost. As fast as she moved, I felt that she was waiting for me, not showing the true nature of her speed.

And then the gunshots came. Pain, hot and terrible tore at my right shoulder and chest. The ground came up to meet me, hard, as if a giant's hand had socked me high in the back and knocked me spinning. "Tebre, go on!" I screamed, scrambling on my knees, then falling again. "Go!" I heard the mushy garble in my own voice this time as the truth of it filled my mouth and bled out across my t-shirt.

I rolled over and abruptly found myself staring at the shivering shape of the weapon that suddenly pressed near my forehead, right between my eyes. The woman looking down at me was blond, with cold gray eyes and thin lips. Her finger tightened on the trigger.

Chapter 24

Every time one of your Children of God as you call them falls, I feel it. No, not with regret or pain or anything quite so poetic. I simply note that one more data source has gone offline. It is a factual loss, but once noted, I no longer grieve as I have seen Samu'el do. I don't understand such things—I am lessened, not him. But he is the one moved to tears.

Conversations with Nuress
Spirit Marga Archives

Panting with fear and pain, I looked up into the woman's round face. "If you pull that trigger, you'll all die with me. I won't be able to stop it."

She hesitated, her eyes wavering for a moment. "You're just a human, getting his kicks with that rogue CoG."

I gripped my bleeding shoulder and could feel the blood's slick warmth between my fingers. "What?" I played half-heartedly with the designation she had used. CoG—Children of God. Lovely how words could objectify and dehumanize so efficiently.

She shoved the gun harder against my forehead, but I hardly felt it. Everything was curiously swimming now, sound, sight, even the smell of her fading in and out. "You know. The big woman. She's a rogue, won't come in for registration. You think we weren't taught how dangerous these forest CoGs are? We hunt them and the sympathizers like you. Shoot to kill. Even the Margas know about it; they just look the other way. Or take notes behind the trees."

I could hear enough of the fanatic in her then. "Pull your trigger," I said. "I think you'll find your toy doesn't work anymore." To my consternation, she grinned and did pull it.

Nothing happened except the small hiccough of the gun's movement against my skin.

She pulled the weapon back and looked at it with a dull sort of surprise. "Well, I'll be damned," she said. "What in the hell are you?" She whistled to her team members. Moments later, three others joined her. "The fishy and the feline have gone tracking," one man said, his Northern accent thick. "Whatcha got there, Sussie?"

"Don't know. Put my gun out of commission. Any of yours work?"

Triggers clicked uselessly, and then of course, their eyes turned to me with a kind of wonder. It did not seem to occur to them that I could shut them down just as easily. I could feel the nausea starting, the almost euphoric shock from the wound I had taken beginning to fade.

"What about him, then?"

Sussie slung her rifle. "Maybe he knows how to get to that rogue."

"Just met," I said. "And I'm...not going to...help you."

"Yeah? Then you can just bleed to death." She reached for her hip, pulling out an ugly toothed knife. "Bet you can't shut this down, you damn CoG."

I shut my eyes, jaw knitting around the pain. "Don't." I said. "You've got... to stop."

I heard her crouch near me, felt her fingers knit in my hair as she exposed my neck. The cold bite of steel rested against my pulse. "I don't gotta do nothing," she said. I looked into her eyes and hated her. I wanted her to end, to fly apart. And in that moment, I felt it go out of me, the shadow of death. I took only one breath and four bodies hit the ground without a sound, and her knife slid harmlessly off my chest.

I dragged myself to my feet somehow, trying hard not to look at them. I was so cold, and the ground rocked unevenly beneath my feet. I realized, then, that I was not alone. The two Children of God had returned, and stared at me in raw shock. "Just go," I said, feeling the blood seeping through the fingers that cradled the front of my shoulder. So much blood. And a hole, where there should have been flesh. Why was I still conscious? "For God's sake, just go," I heard myself saying to them, but it was barely more than a whisper.

They did, the cat-faced man urging the sea child away from me.

I backtracked, dimly thinking I should use the blanket I'd dropped to staunch the flow of blood. But my feet felt thick and unreal and before I quite knew what had happened, I hit the ground. The jarring finally pulled a scream out of me, though I could feel myself faintly amused and dismayed by the sound. I lay with my cheek in the moss and leaves, blinking.

I had killed again.

I was dead again.

I had always been dead.

The hand that touched my back was gentle but I still startled with it. Tebre gathered me up as she might a child, her rich red eyes compassionate and fearful at once. "Ianto-seeker? How did you..."

I rested my head on her chest. "I told you my gift was not as civilized as your own."

"Civilized?" She giggled a bit, smoothing my hair back from my face. Her hand then covered my wound, the sharp claws biting a little into tattered skirt of skin around it. She hummed to herself, almost like a cat purring by the fire. I could feel the vibration around the edges of the ripped flesh, a rippling of coolness and a gentle dragging sensation. The pain eased. I hadn't been aware of how hot and ugly and deep the pain had gone until it stopped.

She smoothed back my hair again. "The bullet went all the way through. It is not all healed within, but the bleeding has stopped. We will wait for a time, and I will try again. I am not so good a healer when I am angry," she confided, "or scared."

I nodded against her chest, my eyes closing.

"Sleep, yes, sleep Ianto-Seeker," she whispered. "You are watched over."

Chapter 25

This part might seem strange. I feel like there are several personalities within Ianto, one like an organizing principle, several other more peripheral. But he was kind, and despite what I had seen him do to the hunters, I never feared being by his side.

Debriefing Notes
Subject: Tebre, Binder

I woke with light streaming into the reservation cabin. I sneezed a couple of times, tensing against a pain that didn't, remarkably, come. Everything in the tiny bedroom had a fine and even layer of dust coating it, from the small built-in desk to the half-opened and slatted closet.

Tebre immediately came to the door with the sound of my sneeze. "Better?" she asked. She was holding something steaming in her hand. "I've made pine tea. We're lucky...the power cells are still working here. That's unusual. Would you like some?"

I nodded. "Anything to eat?"

"A simple tuber stew. Bland, but then that would be best for you, yes, being a seeker and all?"

"Yes," I said. I started to push aside the covers and realized I was quite naked. I looked up at her amused grin, frowning.

"Too much blood makes you too easy to track. I left your clothes in the woods, along with your blanket."

"Which means you...."

"Carried you birthday-naked through the woods?" Tebre tipped her head, eyes twinkling. "Yep." And she disappeared from the room.

I got up, and shut the door firmly. The closet didn't offer much, just a few pants and an old brown and dusty sweater. I pulled my selections on. The sweater was too short in the sleeves, but serviceable. The pants, too, were short and loose. I lucked out, found a much-used fabric belt back in the corner of a drawer and cinched it tighter around my waist. Reasonably covered, I made my way out to what doubled as the kitchen and dining area.

Tebre perched on the edge of the table; I could see the chairs would not have managed her height well. As it was, she could reach up and touch the ceiling without fully extending her arm. She cast me an appraising eye, one eyebrow raised high.

"Don't," I warned her.

She put up three fingers, warding me off. "I will say nothing." But she grinned. She waved me to the small bowl of stew near the sink. I took it, leaning back against the grimy countertop. The food was warm and bland as she had said. But for me, a fast gone on for over four days, the meal was perfect. I ate quietly, slowly, hoping it would all stay down and she seemed content to merely watch me.

When I was done, and I had found serviceable sandals and socks to wear, she drew me outside. The sun was slanting through the trees, creating ribbons of light. The cabin was isolated, with no other buildings visible. The faint tracing of a driveway petered off to the west, curving into the ferns and deadfall. "I am not sure what to do with you now, Ianto." She looked longingly toward the woods. "I do not stay long in any place since the Others have come hunting us, and making our way to the highway seems imprudent just now."

"Us?" I asked, catching her tone.

"We are still many, here in the woods. Not all Children follow the Margas or the Emperium.

The outsiders have been scouring these woods off and on for years now. A number of us have been killed and parts of them taken away, but I do not know to what end. We harm no one, and yet they come."

I sat down on a large boulder, what may have once been a part of a Zen garden, now gone wild and wispy. *Parts of them* echoed in my mind, and I had to suppress a shudder. "The hunters said they were here with the Marga's knowledge." I put my hands on my knees, thinking while she crouched, toying with a stick. "How have you lived here for so long?"

"I run and evade them. Sometimes I have watched from above and from under the cover of the brush. Mostly, they are merely inconvenient. It is an easy thing for me, this play, but not for all the Children. Some fight when cornered, some fall and cry. Each according to their way in the world, I suppose. But I have learned to stay away from the cabins, except for more than a day. To leave things untouched as much as possible. So we cannot stay here and give them wind of us."

I nodded, understanding.

"None of us have killed so many at once before," Tebre said carefully. "Do you think they will fear us and stay away now?"

I lowered my head. "As you say, it depends on their way in the world. It might deeply anger whoever has ordered the killing here. Or it might make them more cautious I suppose. It could change the pattern of how they hunt." I felt the deaths again, keenly. No choice, I thought to myself, and they were murderers themselves. But it was a small consolation.

"Not knowing is wise. It will keep us awake," Tebre said, baring her teeth in a feral smile. "So, Ianto, do I try to take you back to the road or do you wish to come into the wilderness with me?"

I looked into her red eyes, the dark stillness of her, the predator and the healer dancing there together. "I'll stay with you for a time," I said. "I owe you my life, which is something not to be taken lightly by a monk of the Spirit Marga."

"Monk?" she laughed. "Truly?"

"I'm afraid so," I returned.

"Then perhaps your God will watch over us. We will go and find the forest Children and you will say your blessings over them. They will laugh at you, as I do, but perhaps it will make you feel better, yes?"

I looked down at my fresh scrubbed hands, half expecting to see my own blood still there. Or the blood of the ones I had killed. "I don't think I will easily find the ear of God," I answered.

Chapter 26

It stood to reason that if something could control the Children of God, then that technology could be adopted for use by the Margas themselves. However, attempts to route specific instructions through their nanotech met with unexpected results. Sometimes the Children went comatose. Sometimes, it seemed as if they were trying to do two separate things at once, and both badly. Sometimes they became not so much controlled as more malleable and impressionable. We continue to struggle with this technology today.

Science Marga Tech Journal

I blew into my hands, rubbing them briskly. For nearly three weeks, we'd walked the forest. She had shown me the remains of several reservations, now empty. We found fresh blood in one, and went away quiet for the entire day. Occasionally, we crossed paths with other Children of God, but did not linger with them.

Another afternoon was fading now, cold and damp.

Tebre smiled at me from where she crouched, tending a small, almost smokeless fire next to the base of a tall cedar. "The tubers did not warm you up?"

I glanced at my dirty hands. "They were fine, although I tend to like my root veggies a little less rare." I said then realized how rude I was being. "I'm OK, Tebre."

"I don't feel the cold so much," she noted. She raised her head, her red eyes narrowing and her breath suddenly tight and high in her chest. She gently snuffed the tiny fire with her foot, her eyes on the tall ferns and underbrush.

I moved slowly, carefully to her side. "Company?" I whispered below my breath.

"Yes. But what sort I do not know yet," she murmured back. We edged back from the remains of our fire, sliding beneath the ferns and bracken. I was struck again a how big she was, nearly seven feet high, and how quietly she could move. Next to her, I was clumsy and uncoordinated.

It felt like a great deal of time passed before he came out along the deer trail. Beside me, I could feel Tebre tightened, but not with fear.

152

Red eyes turned our way, dark hair swinging over his broad shoulders. His face was long, blending into a solid and squared chin. Two hunting daggers adorned his simple belt, and he wore jeans and a gray flannel shirt of all things. Leather would have suited him better.

She stood up and I had no choice but to rise with her.

The other Binder's hand went to his daggers immediately, his head cocked in that strange bird-like movement that Tebre used. He measured us, crouched, ready to flee or fight.

Tebre opened her empty hands to him. "We do not hunt you," she said. "I am Tebre and this is Ianto, a monk of the Spirit Marga."

"Monk?" The tall creature straightened slowly, his eyes curious but still cautious. He looked me over carefully then studied Tebre with more than a clinical interest. "You're like me," he said. "There are so very few of us."

Tebre beckoned to him, her long fingers curving the air like a harpist. "Indeed. Come. Speak with us."

He considered her for a moment. He shook his head and pointed beyond us. "Night will fall soon. I have a small cave. It's warm and safe.

Come with me and I can offer you a safer rest. My name," he added, "is Warren."

I shifted uncomfortably.

"You *and* your monk can come," he said with a small smile to me.

Tebre looked at me, then. "I believe we will be safe, Ianto-seeker." And I could see in her eyes the deep desire to go with him then. To be with one who wore the kind of body she did, who stood so tall in the darkening woods, perhaps the other half of her soul come to her at last. I could only nod.

We set out, the darkness beginning to make the going hard. I jogged along behind them; they set a fair pace, talking with great animation, which meant they were intentionally waiting for me. Over this deadfall, avoid those blackberry trailers, duck the low slung branch, the darkness making depth and distance a difficult judgment, we paced through the forest. And yet, here I felt a weird twist of peace, even trailing two Binders through the dark, navigating the rising hills. I accepted them. They accepted me. No habit, no history. Just a simple man sliding on the wet leaves and mud.

I was tired and winded when we drew up at last. The forest looked like it had for an hour, shadowed and still. Warren stepped off the faint trail, and started to climb the steep hillside. We followed him as he angled carefully up and to the left. And then, it was as if the hill itself pulled him in.

Tebre and I stopped, startled. Warren's head popped up from the ground. "Drop in carefully; the cave is down through this shaft."

Tebre went first, dropping cautiously into the hole in the ground. I crouched beside the open wound in the earth, and could see nothing but blackness. Warren's face appeared suddenly and I nearly startled back. "Do you need help? It is a short fall for us but more so for you."

"No," I said firmly, throwing my legs over the edge of the hole. I pushed off, and landed on my feet. Warren reached out to steady me. The ground here was firm. I extended my hand out in the darkness, feeling the closeness of the damp walls and roots. Warren plucked at my arm, startling me. "This way, monk."

I let myself be led along a narrow passage, so narrow in fact that at times I had to turn sideways, and still the earth and roots scraped at me, but only for perhaps fifteen or twenty steps. I could feel Tebre behind me now, her hand occasionally reaching to touch my shoulder.

Then I felt as if space had opened around me. "Stand here," Warren said to us both.

A moment later, a small fire sprang up, the shadow of the male Binder feeding it gently. He motioned us to join him then, as the light grew. The cave was very strange, its surface almost perfectly smooth and granite gray. The floor was dirt, though, and dry. Not a large space, it spanned only fifteen feet or so, and the ceiling hovered just a hand-width above Tebre's head.

Warren looked up at us. "When the Great Reckoning happened," he said, "my father created three caves like this in the deep wood. He was afraid for me, and wanted a place where I could hide if necessary. It was good foresight. He cut this from the rock." He gestured around him.

"Warren in a warren," I said softly to myself.

He laughed, though I had not intended him to hear me. "Indeed."

"Where is your father now?" I asked.

Warren stood then, moving toward the woodpile at the back edge of the cave. "He was hunted for helping the free Children of God. He's dead now, as is my mother." He piled a few thick branches in the crook of his arm, his movements quick and sure.

"I mourn your loss," Tebre said quietly. "And thank you for your hospitality."

"We are the Children of God," he said simply. "How can we not help our own?"

He laid the logs next to the fire, dropping to the ground, and I came to sit with them. He considered me, through the flame. "What are you besides a monk?"

"A breaker of things," I answered. Tebre smacked at me, a quick flick of her fingers, telling me to behave.

"Oblique," Warren chided, "but then, you are Spirit Marga. Tell me, then, how are you a Child of God?"

I told him, then, how my gift had manifested. Tebre filled in what I could not, how I killed the hunters and how she had in turn healed me. I felt the heaviness of it again. Walking in the woods, I could pass through the pain as through fog, but sitting still, with two sets of deepest red eyes looking at me, the darkness in myself stirred and nibbled at my guts.

"He was surprised," Tebre said, "when I did not attack him and lick at his blood to torment him." She giggled then, like a small child. "Can you imagine?"

Warren tipped his head, but I could see in that moment he could imagine it. His eyes looked at me in deep speculation, and I swallowed quickly and looked away. "You have met others like us," he said, gesturing to Tebre.

"Not here. And not like you," I said.

He looked at me quizzically.

"I don't think you would understand."

"He has visions," Tebre explained. "Our kind have appeared to him in dreams, and they are very different from us, or from me anyway." She grinned again, and shifted on the earth.

"Tebre," I said quietly, shaking my head.

Warren settled onto his side, his long legs outstretched along the edge of his fire pit. He propped his head in his hand, the firelight catching the red of his eyes. "I have tasted the blood when I heal," he said casually.

Tebre went very still beside me, her face a mix of wonder and revulsion.

"I can heal with the hand, or with the blood-way."

I watched him there, the picture of wild languor, the predator stretched out by the fire.

"You don't seem driven by it," I observed cautiously.

"Not right now," he said.

"Now you are the one being cryptic," I said.

"Warrens and crypts," Tebre muttered to herself. "And blood."

Warren smiled at her. "What God made you so light of spirit?" he asked.

Tebre tossed her hair back from her shoulder. "The same one that made you, I suppose. And Ianto. Answer his question." Her eyes flashed a bit then, her eyebrows drawing together.

"I have been driven by the blood, after my father's death. I hunted the hunters. I took my revenge on them many times over. It is done now." His eyes glowed then, feral and cold. "The lust is still here, but I am its master."

"For now," I said softly. The fire crackled and Tebre jumped a bit. Warren grinned at her.

"Your monk is a little afraid of me, I think," he said. "But you?"

"Curious only," she said, her voice low in her throat.

"That's a good and prudent place to start," he replied.

Chapter 27

Populations are best controlled through the media of their own choosing. While not as wholly predictable as closed-lab single participant indoctrination techniques, the group mind is quite malleable in its own way.

Anthology of Socio-Religious Indoctrination Protocol Studies
Nasha McKinney, Ed.

I woke to a kind of darkness that pressed upon my eyes. I smelled wood smoke and sweat and for a moment my heart hammered in my chest as I tried to remember where I was. Then the long night of talk and falling off to sleep came to me. I finally remembered Warren's cave and the warmth of a fire now dead.

"Tebre?" I whispered. In the cave I had no sense of day or night, but I felt rested and more than ready to leave the bowels of the earth. I heard her stir, off to my right, and cautiously reached my hand out. I found her foot, and gave it a little shake. "Tebre. Wake up."

Tebre growled a little, low in her throat. I could hear her rustle in the darkness. "Warren?" she asked, her voice husky with sleep. More rustling, but no voice greeted us. "Warren?" she called a little louder. My eyes scanned the darkness, but nothing was discernable.

"He must have gone out. The passage is over here somewhere."

"Over where somewhere?" I asked. A hand came out of the darkness and grabbed my wrist.

"This way," Tebre said.

We shuffled across the cave floor, my hand reaching out to touch the wall. Tebre found the narrow pathway to the opening first. She tugged me in behind her, past the clinging roots and earth. She stopped after a few feet. "There's a wall in front of me," she said, an edge of panic in her voice. I strained to reach past her; in the narrow passageway we couldn't stand side by side. My hand touched what felt like cold metal. I knelt awkwardly, trying to feel if it went all the way to the floor. "How high does it go?" I asked.

"I can't touch the top," she replied. Suddenly, she threw herself forward, battering at the obstruction. It rang back her blows with a hollow sound, but didn't budge.

"This obviously wasn't an accident. Warren locked us in here," I said. The walls pressed tight around me, and I could feel the beginnings of panic. I edged back down the corridor toward the main cave. After a few more sounds of Tebre tackling the wall, she, too, returned to the cave. I slid down the wall, hugging my knees to my chest.

"What is he doing?" she asked quietly. The fabric of her clothes rustled as she joined me on the floor.

"I don't know. He's a blooded Binder, and from what I know of them, he may not do what you expect him to."

We lapsed into silence, our shoulders touching, and stared out into the darkness.

I don't know how much time passed. Tebre, for the first time I had known her, remained silent and contained. Finally, we heard the whisper of movement in the corridor, and then the sounds of the barrier moving. Footsteps padded in the dirt and suddenly a light flared in our faces. We both threw up our arms, blinded. "There you are," Warren said.

Tebre was on her feet in flash of movement, striking him in the chest with both hands. The flashlight went spinning into the dirt. Through fast blinking eyes, I could see she had pushed him clear to the wall. "Why did you lock us in here?" she demanded.

Warren grasped her wrists and deftly spun her around, hiking one arm up behind her back, nearly bending her back against him. He leaned close to her ear. "I wasn't locking you in, I was locking other things out," Warren growled. And he released her with a not so gentle shove. He pulled a backpack around to his hands and shook it. "Breakfast," he said. "And you're welcome."

He restarted the fire, and we joined him, I for one feeling foolish. He passed out apples and a handful of nuts to us while we watched him silently. He looked at us then, in the firelight. "I had to go back for these, to my other cave. You were both sleeping, so I locked this place down. I'm sorry if I frightened you."

Tebre nodded her grudging forgiveness. I looked down from his face.

When I glanced back up, he was watching me carefully. "These other Binders in your vision, they made a very deep impression on you, I see. But I'm flesh and blood, monk. Don't presume to think you know me."

I met his gaze then. "I can't change what I have experienced. I will try to keep those things separate from you. But please understand, I have never seen the level of pure brutality that the other Binders possessed and if you are blooded...."

"I have told you, that was a long time ago." He looked back into the fire. "Yes. I admit it. To heal in the blood way is like consummating a love, an act of sexual depth and feeling for me. But the act also was full of hatred and conquest. It is a powerful drug. I know that. But as I said, I have control over it now." He glanced at Tebre. "She could be just as your visions, but you don't fear her."

"He has no reason to; he knows me now," Tebre said quietly. "But it was an earned trust."

Warren smiled sadly, poking the fire with a long stick. "Fair enough." He shoved the stick deeper in the fire then drew his long legs to his chest. "So where will you two journey now?"

"I have taken him along the ridge country," she said. "I will make a slow circuit along the ocean front; it is a beautiful place when the fog is out and the wind is high."

Warren nodded, absent-mindedly. "Beautiful, but dangerous. The hunters come in from the seaside. They have been setting traps there. Go carefully."

"You won't come with us?" Tebre asked quietly.

He looked at her, his head tipped to one side. "I am not a monk, Tebre. Be sure of what you are asking of me."

She smiled shyly at him.

I cleared my throat. "I'm going up to the surface. It was a long night, and well...I am experiencing the urge of certain biological functions."

Tebre laughed aloud, and Warren smirked at me.

They joined me a bit later, looking askance at my dirty sweater and pants. "Harder climb for me as well as a harder drop," I said with a shrug. The wind was moving through the trees with great purpose, and here and there, a bough dropped to earth. Tebre shook her hair in the wind, her lips pulled back from her teeth in savage joy. "I love the wind," she declared. I noticed Warren's eyes on her breasts, and turned discretely to the side.

"My farthest cave is on your route," Warren said. He pointed at an angle away from the ridgeline. "Perhaps six or seven hours walk. I will give us shelter this evening. Dark is falling sooner now."

I nodded. "Good. It's a wild day for a hike, but I'm up for it." The wind shoved at me, even here in the deep woods, and the fir trees roared.

And so we hiked along another faint deer trail, the two Binders talking and laughing ahead of me, myself lost to thoughts and the push of the wild wind.

We came across the bodies just after mid-day, four Children of God.

It was hard to tell their genotype; animals had been chewing on the corpses for days and the smell drove us back. Two were totally missing their heads, the others more or less intact although one had a hole in her chest where her heart used to be. I backed off, fled down the trail a bit and wretched what was left of breakfast into the underbrush.

Tebre and Warren came up the trail more slowly, Tebre very pale and Warren with his red eyes narrow and hooded. I must have looked awful, because Tebre went to me at once, put a hand on my shoulder and nodded her sympathy into my miserable face.

"You see, now, how they leave us. Take pieces of us, and leave the rest to rot. Perhaps they run tests on the bits of us that cannot fight back."

Warren ground his teeth, quite audibly. "And you look at me as if I was a monster."

"I still don't understand what they are doing here, on the reservation lands," I said. "It makes no sense. This doesn't feel like something a Marga would allow. This has to be something different."

"How would you know, really? What would a monk understand about the larger world?" Tebre asked softly.

"Enough to know that the Margas work together, and Spirit Marga would not condone this." But even as I said it, I wondered in the pit of my stomach. The brutality, no, but the issue of control was very important to both Margas. And the reservation Children of God were not under anyone's control. An idea occurred to me. "What if you registered with the Spirit Marga?" I asked carefully. "Reclaim all this as Spirit Marga reservation lands. They'd be duty-bound to protect you then," I said.

Warren looked at me deeply then shook his head. "I will not be owned."

"I'm not owned," I said. "I'm standing here, am I not, by my own free will?"

He didn't take his eyes from my face. "Your own free will? Really?"

I had to look away then because he was right. Without Jean, it was highly unlikely I would be standing with Binders and the corpses of Children of God in the deep forest.

He nodded, seeing my gaze waver. "They have convinced you that your life is your own, but it is not. You and your kind are bought and sold on a whim. And whoever let you out to wander for a while is probably closer than you think." He reached out and took Tebre's hand. "We will not live long free; of this my father knew the truth. I for one will die before I register with Spirit Marga or Science Marga or even the damned North Emperium."

"There must be a way to stop this. I'm a Child of God, too. Those corpses back there were part of me and I of them," I said.

Warren laughed then, low and with a critical edge. "In truth, you are a danger to us, monk. I have seen the hunters with their registered CoGs as they call them. Hunting dogs, all. Who is to say that you are not one of them, sent in to gather us together and die like them? You say you fear me? Then know how much I fear you. I would see you to the highway, and gone from here."

Tebre pulled her hand gently away from Warren, but her eyes were troubled. "It's true, Ianto, that the first hunting party fell on us far too quickly and well."

I stared at her as if for the first time. "Where are these ideas coming from? They may have caught the tracker device, but that is broken now and growing moss somewhere," I said. "You know I wouldn't hurt you, and we have had a clear three weeks in these woods. If they could track me, they would have come."

"I know you have not hurt me," she agreed. "But beyond that, I know nothing of the reach of the Margas or Emperium. I'm a simple healer." Her eyes asked me to convince her, but there was precious little I could say that would do that. She looked up at Warren, and as her face softened a little, my own heart sank.

"I'm not a hunting dog, as you put it," I said. I felt a flush of anger toward her. How had Warren, in the span of a day, cracked a three-week friendship so easily? "I only came for a fast and we got caught up with the hunters. I stayed because I wanted to know you, Tebre. I wanted to...to see if the nightmares were simply dark dreams." I looked into her strange red eyes. "I'll go, if that's what you wish. Of course, I'll go."

"But truly, that would not be the best use of you," Warren said softly.

How quietly they came from the forest, one of the Seafolks, two wolfish beings, nearly as tall as the Binders with long snouts and lips rippling back from teeth. Each Were stood just behind my shoulder, the flat-eyed Seachild took her place by Warren. Tebre, startled, reached for her dagger. And the Seachild, with a flick of her finger, sent a single shimmering quill into Tebre's throat.

She staggered a step, her gaze wide-eyed with shock, and then she dropped hard onto the wet leaves and mud.

I froze there, trembling.

Warren cocked his head at me then glanced down at Tebre. "She will sleep for a while, and I will give her the antidote and tell her a story to ease her mind." His eyes came back up more slowly. "You, I would use for bait. Better than sending you back with knowledge of us." He drew his backpack off and pulled out my damaged tracker. "My father was very good at teaching me to fix things, monk. I can fix this. And they will come for you, and we will kill them. And they will send more, and I will kill them, too."

I swallowed, feeling the hot presence of the Weres just behind me. "The people who would come for me are not Science Marga, Warren. My Marga will mean you no harm until you hurt them and then more than these simple hunting parties would track you down. They protect their own." I took a step toward him, and I could hear the Were's shift, preparing to haul me to the forest floor. "Please, I'm not just threatening you with this. I don't want their blood on your hands. Nor yours on mine."

"You have told me about your ability to turn things off, organic and no. But I am guessing you do not have the control to kill us without killing Tebre, too."

I knit my jaw then, my own eyes hard and hot. "Is this something you want to find out?"

"But you see, I have no need of either of you, not really. Because, in the end, I have this." Warren cradled the tracker in his huge palm. "You are simply an added benefit." And without the antidote, Tebre's breathing will slow in a day and she will die. The Seachild is her own antidote. Kill the Seachild, you kill Tebre, too. Try to kill me and leave the Seachild alive, and rescue Tebre, she will kill you."

I shook then, with rage.

He pocketed the tracker, and moved very close to me. I craned my neck, looking up at him as a child might look up into the face of a parent in defiance. "I miss humans," he said softly. "And you smell of both human and Child of God. That is a heady thing." He dropped his lips close to the edge of my left ear, and I jerked with the sting as his teeth drew blood. Behind me, one Were growled and half-yipped in amusement as Warren licked the wound and healed it.

Chapter 28

Until you apply pressure to a given subject, you will never understand the extent of what he or she is capable of. But then, you must accept that the pressure may change the subject so entirely that all future behavior paradigms must be adjusted. As the subject changes, so must you, in turn, change. All professional religious have known this as an immutable law.

Behavior Modification for
the Armed Services
Spirit Marga Publications

They half dragged me to a small field just up the path, and tied my hands overhead to a thick tree branch. Warren ripped my shirt away from my chest, laid open a long, red cut from my shoulder and across my ribs with the tip of his knife. I gasped and shuddered in the damp cold, my jaws aching with barely contained rage and pain. Warren didn't say a thing, just smiled showing the edges of his teeth.

Tebre lay at my feet, her breath rising and falling with smooth regularity. I could feel the individual fibers of my bindings. It would be so easy to rip them away. But part of me was frozen, afraid to show what control I could bring to bear. And even if I won free, Tebre might have to suffer for me. So I stood shivering, the blood tickling my belly, and watched as the Children of God faded into the underbrush, waiting.

Warren had not fixed the tracker. He preferred to let the blood scent draw the hunting parties instead. When I was of no further use, the tracker would be repaired and his work would continue. I could feel his eyes on me, in the underbrush, calculating the risk I posed to them against his bloodlust for the hunters.

I leaned my head against my own arm. The wind still howled and the branch tugged painfully at the ropes that wrapped around my wrists. I could feel the roots of the tree beneath me, could run the lines of veins in Warren's skull, could even, with a little more concentration, feel the inner the finest threads in twists of the bindings.

Wait, something in me counseled. *Stand it and wait.*

And then, like a spark of sun, he was there, just off to my side and back, the golden shadow of an elf. I could almost feel the wisps of his hair tickling across my neck. "Blooded Binder? I thought you knew better," he breathed into my ear.

I closed my eyes in answer, my face buried in my arm.

"Still, two Weres, a Seafarin and a Binder, walking together. I have never seen such a thing before." I could feel his hand then, on my back. I trembled with his touch as much as the cold and pain. "So I will give you a word of advice, friend. Help them."

I turned toward him then, his brilliant blue eyes meeting mine with intensity and something like kindness. "Help them?" I asked, my voice cracking. "He fed on me. He's using Tebre. He'll kill whatever or whoever comes into this field. Why in God's name should I help him?"

"So, you do speak," he whispered. He was right; we had never communicated like this before, face to face and our words between us clear and biting. "They have been broken by those who hunt them," he said softly. "They aren't like my Binders, are they? They have had everything taken from them by these hunter beings. You have ever held me together. Hold them."

"Kill for them?" I murmured. "You're asking me to kill for them? I'm a monk. I don't kill, not like this."

"Can't a monk be a sword of God?" he asked. "And if you do not help them, do you possibly turn away from your God?" He placed his hand against my face and I shuddered. His touch was warm and sensual. "I am a shadow here. But I see into you, and I will tell you what I have learned in all my long years at play. The way out is to stop being the slave and become the sword. Or you will die here, in these damp woods, a principled but very dead monk. And I fear there is no Hall of Becoming waiting for you." He smoothed back my hair, his blue-stoned ring glinting coolly. "Are these hunters not your enemies as well?"

"If the hunters are Spirit Marga, I can't...." I began. He put a finger to my lips, his eyes soft now.

"You will know if those who come are your friends. You will know." And then he faded and I nearly cried out with his passing.

The baying of the dogs started far away, a lonely counterpoint to the wind at my back. The sound built until two sleek animals burst from the underbrush, half-dragging their humans behind them. Two more hunters ran, guns at ready.

I reached out to the dogs straining across the wet field, the men stopping, bringing their weapons up. I could feel the heartbeat of the Weres, racing in anticipation, the slow and steady beat of Warren and the fluttering four beat tap of the Seafarin. And I reached with the wind, and entered into the hunters.

I broke the dogs, cringing at their weak whimpers. Then I broke the weapons.

The Children of God broke from their cover, racing from the underbrush. Muzzles snapped up, even as one of the Weres leaped high in the hair, his yellowed claws raking downward. The hunter, a tall man himself, tightened his finger on the trigger. Nothing happened. And then the Were hit him high in the chest with a sound like a watermelon striking pavement.

I turned my face into my arm.

I couldn't shut out their screams, and the silence afterward was just as terrible. When I finally opened my eyes, Warren stood mid-way out in the clearing, hands resting on his hips, looking at me with eyes wide and a little accusing. The Seafarin woman hovered at his elbow.

The wind howled as Warren considered me and then moved through the grasses and tangled berry vines. I lifted my head, the ropes chafing at my wrists. When he came near, he cocked his head to the side. "Why?" he asked.

"Why what?" I asked. My bare torso ached with the cold, the thin line of my wound burned.

"You broke their weapons, didn't you? Why?"

"Because I am a Child of God and you have born enough pain at the hand of those like them." I said. "I will help you, Warren, but out of my own volition and not because you threaten me or Tebre. But I won't kill them. If it is death you want, you'll have to do that."

"Just like that," Warren said, his eyes narrowed.

"Just like that," I returned. "Tebre and the ones like you deserve your freedom, deserve to be able to make choices about how you live. But know this. If you turn a hand against Tebre or me again, I will kill you. I've already broken my vows not to kill. If I have to, I will do it again. Are we clear?"

"A man trussed up like dead deer threatens me?" Warren answered, smiling into my face.

"Not a threat, Warren. You see what I can do. You begin to see the control I have at my disposal. I'm getting more accurate all the time. I'm simply speaking the truth." And I sent my mind into the bonds holding me, and they frayed away, setting me free.

Warren grinned at me in amusement, lips pulling back from black and pointed teeth.

Chapter 29

We see each other through the smoky glass of our own experiences and expectations. How wonderful it would be to start each day without either, and perhaps with a basic trust in the goodness of everything and everyone we meet. But we ate of the tree, we self-reflect, and in the end, that lonely gazing pool catches us forever.

Reflection of the Real
Liam Hollander

I stood with a bowed head over the eight new graves. It had been our tenth battle. The others, seven hunters, had come to their end in the cold autumn rain in various messy ways. I always insisted on the graves, rather than leaving them to the elements. I reasoned with Warren that they would stand testament to those hoping to hunt in the forest of the Children of God. He mostly tolerated the process because the other Children found it was a way to seek a kind of absolution for the blood on their hands. They were taking their rest now, talking in loose knots of two or three. Fourteen Children of God, Warren's army.

And mine, I supposed.

Tebre was sitting under a tree, her knees drawn up and her brow furrowed. She took the deaths the hardest, every cell in her body screaming for her to heal the fallen. She, like myself, would not participate in the fights, but was a wonder at healing the Children of God who were injured. Warren quietly refused to heal on his own, but would often stand at her back, his hand on her shoulder, supporting her if the injury was severe. I had even seen them bring life back into bodies I was sure were dead.

I dropped down beside her, but she didn't look up at me. "So many put to earth, Ianto, and they still keep coming. Why?"

I leaned my head back against the tree. "They may be offering a price for each of us," I said. "Or they may find it a kind of sport. I don't know."

"We need to catch one," Tebre said softly. "Then maybe we would know. Warren tried in the past, you know, to get one to talk, but said he never got anywhere. I think he just preferred to kill rather than find the reason."

I looked at her, the way the rain pearled in her dark hair. "It's a good idea," I said. "Catch one, try to find out who is sending them or why." I picked up a pinecone, one of the soft, slender kinds with little tufts like tongues protruding from each thumbnail seed. "I hate to admit it, but I think I've been afraid to find out the why."

"I know," Tebre answered.

"Can I ask you something?"

She looked at me then, her deep red eyes holding mine. "Of course."

"Why are you still drawn to Warren, after all you have seen him capable of? You two seem so at odds in this life. And yet..."

She sat quietly for a moment, watching the new graves shed their rainwater into naked earth. Finally, she extended her hand for the pinecone I was holding. I passed it to her. "This cone is full of life, yes? But armored on the outside. When I heal with his hands on my shoulders, I feel what his heart used to be like or could be like." She turned the cone slowly. "There will be a chink someday, and he will let it all come out again."

"Tebre, the blooded Binders are not like you. I don't think he wants to be like you again...the armor goes all the way through. Please, be careful."

"It is in the nature of a healer to be an optimist," Tebre countered with a tired smile.

Warren joined us a moment later, sitting on the other side of Tebre, his red eyes quickly scanning the other Children of God. "A good battle."

"Except for the Shodo," I said.

"Little fluffy things like her should know to stay out of the hand-to-hand fighting. The Weres, the cats, even Seafarin are far better at this kind of work. Still, I suppose part of me admired her courage," Warren replied. He arched his back, stretching.

Tebre turned the pinecone in her fingers, her eyes sad.

"So, Ianto, what now, do you think?" he asked, his eyes keen on mine. I noticed his fingers fidget, his jaw a bundle of muscles, flexing. With each week that passed, his almost feral nature was building. I was glad for Tebre between us, her solid and kind presence mitigating his darkness.

"Tebre and I were talking," I said. "We need to catch one of the hunters, to see if we can figure out why they keep coming even now that they are losing so many. I think if they simply wanted us dead, they'd burn this place to the ground. Or send in gunships, something bigger than the small hunting groups."

"Poorly trained squads, too." Warren scratched at his upper lip. "They take parts of us, when they can kill us," Warren mused. "That has been the mystery to me. What good a head, or a heart, or an arm?"

I shook my head, my eyes on the dirt between my feet. "I think we need to figure it out. Maybe it'll give us a way to take the fight to them."

"Take the fight to them?" Tebre asked, abruptly dropping the pinecone. "Leave the forest?"

"Maybe," I said, with a shrug.

"I won't leave the forest," Warren said tightly.

"Nor I," soothed Tebre. They shared a small smile between them and I felt a wave of uneasiness.

"Well, until we catch a hunter, it's all conjecture." I stood, brushing pine needles and damp earth from my heavy canvas pants. "Do you think you can do it?" I asked Warren.

"Of course. The hunt will be a delight, Monk." The big Binder laughed, baring his sharp black teeth.

My heart caught at the old title. Monk. Man of God. "Just Ianto, Warren. Just Ianto," I murmured, my eyes falling on the muddy graves.

Chapter 30

It has never been the fact that Nuress could potentially control the Children of God that so vexed me as it does the Margas and Emperium. Of course, we need a central guiding intelligence to coordinate such an army. And of course, there is no way that intelligence could be wholly human. To orchestrate many thousands of life forms, to discern their placement in society and their actions, and never, never to sleep—that is the work a machine. Or a god. But a machine, no matter how intelligent, could never have the long-range insights of a human because it does not clearly see its mortality as we do. And would a god simply find, in the end, it does not care?

Technical Notes
Petrek, Senior Analyst

The Children had been out on the trail for nearly five days before they returned. Two Seafarin and I had just finished a meager evening meal when Tebre emerged from the woods, muddied and grim. The others followed, heads drooping with fatigue. I counted four who had gone who did not return. Warren shoved a human before him with one hand, holding an elegant black compound bow in the other.

"Sit," Warren commanded, and the human dropped to his knees in the mud. His dark hair fell over his face, his hands were bound before him and even from here I could see the open wounds in his wrists. His fatigues were ripped at the knees and he looked more mud than living flesh. His shoulders shook, though with fear or fatigue I couldn't tell.

I came slowly to my feet. "What happened?"

"Different weapons," Warren shook the bow. "They shot from the trees. Clever. This one ran, so he gets to live a while longer." He crouched by the human. "I have enjoyed our journey," and he reached out one hand to the man's shrouded face. The captive twitched away, his breath suddenly ragged.

Tebre came to Warren's side, quietly taking the bow and his arm. "Come and eat, Warren. Ianto will talk to the hunter." She cast me a worried look as she led the other Binder to what was left of the food.

I waited for a moment then hunkered in the mud and leaves in front of the man. "What's your name?" I asked quietly.

The man's head rose. I frowned at his youth and his dark, bruised eyes and the barest beginnings of a beard on his chin. "Vic," he said, as if his throat clutched at his own voice. "My name is Vic." His eyes were wide with fear.

"Vic, I have to ask you a few questions. But I'm not going to hurt you, do you understand?"

He nodded, but his eyes said otherwise.

"Why are you hunting the Children of God?" I asked. I could feel him sizing me up and tried to radiate calmness, stillness. In the end, he sort of slumped and I knew I had won through to him.

"I didn't *know* we were, not right off," he whispered. "Honest to God, I didn't know when I took the job. But then they explained it all to us, and we all felt we had to." He looked up into my face, his eyes pleading.

"The job?" I prodded. "What job? Who offered it and why?"

"Just a holo-posting at the archery club, advertising big game experience. Six hunters, tree blinds, you know, basic stuff. Clear a reservation wolf pack gone bad. Sounded like fun." Vic shook his head. "They um...picked us up at the club and we drove for like a day. We off-loaded at this big hunting lodge. Then they told us what we were really hunting, and why."

I shifted against the earth, my feet cold as always. A small peek of late sunlight wafted its way down to us, catching the edges of needles and branches. "What could they have said to make you hunt the Children of God?" I asked.

"It was the holos they showed us," Vic said. "Killings going on all over the world but especially in the rural areas like the woods here. The CoGs are hunting in packs, doing terrible things. They said it wouldn't be long before they started to hit the cities. Said we needed to kill 'em and get heads and hearts and try to see if others could be fixed up somehow, you know, like maybe their nanotech loads were going wrong again."

He looked up at me, his dark eyes pleading. "I know folks who are CoGs. They're weird but OK. I don't want to have to be afraid of them. If someone can fix them, then I want to help. You know?"

I looked at him in disbelief. "Even if it meant killing?"

He closed his eyes, his face miserable. "Come on," he said at last. "You've felt it. They're not like us. Not really." He paused as if listening to himself then shook his head. "Yeah, well, I thought I could kill them, but ....I couldn't pull my bow, I mean, targets are one thing, but...and then the killing started and the blood and I just ran. I just ran, and that whatever he is clobbered me."

He cast a short glance over his shoulder, his eyes wide and full of fear. "He's like some kind of fuckin' vampire. That thing he does to me..." he started to shake again, his eyes going to the ground. "You got to keep him away from me, OK?" he whispered. "I can't take any more of that shit." I could see the panic starting to rise, and knew I would lose him if that happened.

"He's a Binder," I said, keeping my voice level. "And they aren't all like him. Vic, look at me." The boy's wild eyes came to my own, softened a little. "He won't hurt you anymore, OK?" I tried to smile just a little, but I could feel my stomach knot and had to keep myself from glancing over at Tebre and Warren.

"And what are you doing here?" he asked, his eyes coming back to mine. "I mean, you're like me, your own kind, and I don't see any ropes on you. They said that some humans like you might be prisoners of the CoGs and we were supposed to bring the humans back alive with us. That just fired us up more, you know, go in and save our own kind. How in the hell they ever thought we could do that...I mean, have you ever seen a Were rip a guy..." his eyes started to dart around him, wild and cornered.

"I'm not a prisoner," I said, cutting him off. "I fight as a Child of God because I am one."

"No way," he said, shaking his head. "You're human. You're nothing like these...these creatures."

"They're human, too, at their cores," I said. "You know that; that's why you couldn't kill them. They're not animals, and right now, they are as scared as you. And there are no genetically normal humans with us; it's just another lie they've told you. Did do know there have been hunters in the woods for years, killing them, mutilating them, leaving their corpses to rot in the rain? So they started fighting back, but it's all escalating now. We just need to know why. Anything you tell us, anything at all, is helpful."

"But it was them who started it," Vic cried uncertainly. "If you had seen the holos..."

"Holos can be made up, stories created," I answered, keeping my voice reasonable. "These people never meant anyone any harm, not in the beginning." I reached out to touch Vic's shoulder, but the younger man jerked himself away.

"I don't believe you," Vic said, his voice cracking. "I don't, not after what I saw a couple days ago. No way. They are monsters."

"Who hired you, Vic? Who?" I put just a little steel in my voice, but I wasn't good at it. All I wanted to do was take the poor kid over by the fire, feed him and wrap him in a blanket. Because he was just that, a teenager, really, out for kicks and a few bucks and ending up with more than he had bargained for. "Like I said, just a guy. Um. Redhead, shaved short, you know, military style. Guys mostly up at the cabin, all pretty normal folks."

"Think," I said softly. "Anything that stood out, anything weird or off."

"No. Nothing." Vic swallowed.

"Names? Did you get any names?"

"No, not...I mean, the big redhead who picked us up at the range was called something like Pete maybe. And huh, there was a guy at the lodge called Leland who did most of the talking. Weird name, that's why I remembered it. He did all the map work and sort of drilled us in what we might expect for a few days...."

I stood slowly, and Vic looked up at me from the ground. I'm sure my face was something to behold; I could feel my own cheekbones pushing up through the tension of my face muscles, my eyes hardening as if I had just been hit. Out of the corner of my eye, I saw Warren rise, as well, although Tebre held his hand, anchoring him by the tiny fire.

"You OK?" Vic asked.

"This guy," I whispered. "Light brown skin, black hair, very short cut, very precise speech?"

"Yeah," Vic said. "Yeah, that would be him."

"What Marga are you, Vic?" I asked, fighting to rein my tension in.

"Marga? Not me. Emperium I guess. I mean I've lived in the North all my life."

I nodded. "That'd make sense," I said finally.

Vic watched me uncertainly. "I asked Leland why don't they just call in the troops and raze this place, I mean, you don't send a bunch of archers out to hunt the CoGs if they were such a big threat and he said that it would be worse to panic the populace, that there would be rioting and a military state, and all kinds of stuff I don't get. That we had to keep it quiet, in and out, do our job, get paid, go home." Vic's jaw trembled as he looked sidelong at the fire and the towering

Binder who stood watching with his arms crossed. His gaze came back to my face, pleading. "You gonna let me go home?" he asked.

I looked into his brown eyes, the mix of hope and fear there. I chose not to answer his question. "Do you know how to get back to the lodge where this Leland is?" I asked quietly.

He nodded. "Yeah, I think so...if I can get my hands on even an old-fashioned GPS, I think I can get back from here. It's a long hike, though. Pretty steep going."

I dragged my fingers back through my tangled hair, thinking. It was hard to press past the image of Leland, hard to swallow around the bone of the Spirit Marga and graves and blood. "If you can do that," I said at last, hardly trusting my own voice "and do exactly what I say, I think I can get you home."

Vic nodded, his eyes finally touched with just a flicker of hope.

Chapter 31

From the viewpoint of the casual observer, what we do is miraculous. It is very difficult to convey to others that we do not do the healing. It is not a matter of knowledge or skill or even intent. We simply open a line of communication and get out of its way. The Blooded among us, though, they ride that line, and whatever THAT is that heals also consumes them. Most Binders are simple conduits. The Blooded are possessed.

The Way of the Healer
Collected Binder Writings,
50th Anniversary Edition

I reached for another piece of wood, grimacing at its slimy wetness. "I'm still amazed you folks can tease a fire out of this stuff."

Tebre grinned at me. "We'll make a survivalist out of you eventually," she said. Her own arms were loaded with a considerable bundle of limbs. She abruptly set her damp firewood down, brushing at the smears of mud and debris on her clothing. "So, Ianto, why did you drag me out here alone?"

"There has to be a reason?" I asked. But I smiled at her, letting her know she was right. I loved her perception, her clear vision when it came to reading me. Her fascination with Warren, on the other hand, continued to bother and worry me. I sat my own wood down.

"There is always a reason with you, Ianto," she answered seriously. "Whether you eat so you can live, or sit still so you commune with your God, you always have a reason behind every action."

I shrugged, again unable to argue with her. I looked into her red eyes, as if that would draw her into my own mind and heart. "Vic can lead me to the place where they are training the hunters," I said without preface.

"Really?" she said. "And why would he do that?"

"He wants to live," I said, shaking my head. "Pretty convincing motivation."

"And you promised you could do that for him, let him live, even knowing what he is?" Her voice wasn't really cold, only cautiously disapproving.

"What is he, Tebre?" I asked, allowing a little irritation to creep into my voice. "Really? A scared, brainwashed kid. And a kid who can get me to the root of why all this is happening out here."

Tebre considered me, her head tipped in her birdlike way. "Am I hearing this right? Just you? You wouldn't take the Children of God with you and hit this place?"

I dropped my gaze away then. "It's become more complicated than before."

"Your Marga?" she asked, her eyes narrowing.

I had no choice but to nod. "I'm not sure though. Just a name, a description of someone I might know."

"Even if it was Spirit Marga perpetuating these crimes, what difference would that make?" Tebre asked, her voice a little more chill.

"Because I would have a better chance of effecting some change on a larger scale than the Children of God are able to do," I said. "If it is Spirit Marga, there must be a reason, a philosophical stance they have taken for some purpose. I can address that, Tebre. I'm still a monk of the Marga; I have to try without putting any more Children of God in danger. And without any more lying to the young Emperium citizens from wherever they are being recruited. Walking in there with our small army can't be the way forward. It just can't. There has to be another way. There has to be someone willing to listen to reason."

She raised an eyebrow at me. "Are you a monk with a God complex, Ianto?"

"No," I said, but found myself analyzing my own hubris. "No," I said a little more firmly. "But we are all called to act when we must. Just like you and the other children of God have been forced to act."

"And like Warren? Do your oh-so noble words extend to him as well?" she asked quietly.

"That's not fair," I said. "Warren is a blooded Binder; he has motivations that are much more primal."

"Primal," she said, "doesn't mean *wrong*."

I shook my head, already drained by the contest with her. "No. You're right. And in any case, he has provided a kind of leadership for the Children of God that I could never copy. I can't kill with a clean conscience like he can. In the final analysis, God made him to do one kind of dharma, and he does it. I shouldn't judge him for that. But God has set me on a very different path from his, Tebre. And it's time those paths separated so I do not offend God by not doing the dharma for which I was called into being."

Tebre looked down then. "You're really leaving us, aren't you?"

I stood there in the drizzle and could feel my shoulders sag. "Yes. I'm sorry. But I need your help, because you and I both know Warren will not allow that kid and I to just saunter out of camp. We need just a little head start. I know he'll be on us in a flash once he's figured out what's happened. Just give us that small opening, that chance. Please."

I was surprised to see tears sheening Tebre's eyes. She nodded at me slowly. "I am your friend, Ianto. And perhaps that is my dharma here. You have not convinced me this is wise, but what is important is that you have convinced me you believe it is. I will honor our friendship. Tell me what you have in mind," she murmured.

Chapter 32

There are some who still believe the basic idea is sound: unite humanity through the technology. Break down the lingering barriers of race and age and gender from within, a kind of nanotech-aided enlightenment if you will. But we have never really understood how rooted humankind still is in the paradigm of relational exchange, and how unifying us as a species would awaken the driving urge to remain individual, even if that meant fighting and dying exquisitely alone.

Society's Mirror
Ed. Marvin Tows

Vic looked up into my face, his own dark eyes wild with fear as I sawed through the rope bindings at his wrists. "You're going to what?" he asked, his voice trembling.

I pressed the short knife into his hands, my own touch telling him to be mindful of its edge. I couldn't blame his panic; despite couching what I was about to do in the gentlest of terms, the message was still simple: "I am going to kill you and Tebre is going to resurrect you."

"Don't look at the CoGs," I said, keeping my voice even. I squatted near him, and reached out to turn his face back toward mine forcibly. "It's the only way out Vic. I wish there were some other way, but there isn't. Either this, or it will just be a matter of time before Warren decides to play with you some more. And you know what kind of hell that will be. He could carve on you for weeks before he gets bored, healing the wounds and opening new ones and feeding on you. Is that the route you'd rather take?"

Vic looked at me, a little fire in his eyes. "And you wouldn't stand in his way, is that what you are telling me?"

I smiled at him sadly, my hand on his shoulder. "What makes you think I would fare any better than you?"

"You could kill him."

"I try not to kill people, Vic."

"Except me."

"Yeah," I answered. "But not permanently."

His jaw knit, and I could feel him shaking.

"Angry is good," I said. "You're going to have to hit me now, and you're going to have to draw blood. Understand? Then you have to try to slit my throat. They have to believe that you were going to kill me. Now."

He struck at me a lot faster than I had reckoned, his fist hitting my lip and edge of my nose. I fell back in the mud, stunned, and he was on me in an instant. Archer he might have been, but the kid knew very well how to handle his fists and a blade. For one moment, I was sure he really meant to do it, to cut my throat. He brought the knife in low and controlled but fast. I reached out with my mind and he froze. His eyes widened as the knife dropped from his hand, the blood flooding from his nose and ears. I rolled quickly aside as he fell, face first, onto the ground.

The Children of God were at our side in an instant, their many and varied faces registering surprise. A Seafarin man turned Vic over. The boy's eyes stared up into the tree branches, wide and empty of life. Warren moved more slowly, sauntering from the tiny campfire, Tebre at his shoulder. "Trouble?" he asked casually.

I wiped the blood from my broken lip, not sure I could form words. I shook my head to clear it as I stumbled back to my feet. My jaw ached. "Where did he get the knife?" I demanded, my eyes hard on Warren. I touched my lip gingerly, coming away with a knuckle red with blood.

The big Binder cocked his head at me. "Are you accusing me of something, Ianto-monk?"

Eyes turned toward Warren, speculating.

I spat blood on the ground, letting him stare me down. "No. Of course not." I picked up the knife and tossed it to him. He caught it with a practiced hand, and turned is over. "I don't recognize this blade," he said.

Tebre peered around Warren's shoulder. "It's one of the cooking knives. I thought it had been misplaced at our last camp."

Warren shrugged and tossed the knife back to me. I stepped aside and let it stick in the ground at my feet. "Did you find what you were looking for?" he drawled, but his eyes were sharp, missing nothing.

"No," I answered. I half-closed my eyes, letting my head drop. "No. It was a waste of time. I'll bury him."

"If you want," Warren murmured, and turned back to the fire after casting a warning look around the circle of faces. "Leave the monk alone."

"I'll help you," Tebre said, pitching her voice to be heard. She trotted back to the fire to retrieve a pack shovel as I bent and shouldered Vic's dead weight. I staggered; he was much heavier than I had anticipated. Tebre caught up quickly, tossed the shovel down and with a nod of her head, effortlessly took Vic from me. "I can work as we walk," she whispered. I picked up the shovel where she had dropped it and headed with her into the woods.

"Is anyone following?" I asked quietly.

She shook her head slightly. "You made a mess inside of him, Ianto." Her voice was worried. "Reminds me of the brains of a deer that tangled with a semi-truck."

"Can you heal him?" I asked.

"I don't know," she answered. I swore softly under my breath, and she cast me a reproachful look. "I am trying, but I may need to do something Warren has shown me."

"You're not blooding," I said, surprised at the steel in my voice. "Nobody is worth you using that way of healing. It'll twist you, Tebre."

"Not blooding. A sharing of energy. But I can't do it carrying him. And in a few moments I won't be able to help him."

We had made very little progress into the woods. I looked around, listening into the shadows, but only heard our own breath. "Put him down," I said. I drove the shovel into the dark earth and knelt beside her and Vic.

She put her hands at the younger man's temples. His face was muddy and ashen, the color drained from his lips. His eyes, still open, looked up reproachfully into the sky. "Put your hands on my shoulders. And then get your mind out of the way."

"Get my..."

"Meditate. Open yourself up. Spacious mind, Ianto."

That I knew how to do. I repositioned myself, and let my hands drop on her muscled shoulders. My eyes closed and I felt my heartbeat slow and my breath root deeper in my belly. It was a strange sensation, like a stream was flowing through my hands to her, my mind drifting with only a touch of the witness within. Time stops in such places, at such times. It seemed almost at once that Vic gasped beneath her and started to cry out. She covered his mouth swiftly with her hand, shaking her head in warning. He looked up at us both, his eyes wide and panicked.

Tebre slowly removed her hand. "Are you well, Vic?"

The young man pushed back away from both of us, his eyes blinking rapidly, his lips open and rigid. Sweat stood out on his face, mixing with the mud and debris from his face-first fall into the mud. Tebre started to reach for him, but I caught her arm. She glanced at me and seemed to see my warning look.

"It's OK, Vic. You're back. You're OK," I said.

Vic looked at the two of us, trembling. "Nothing is going to be OK anymore," he whispered. "Nothing."

Chapter 33

The generation born in the years immediately after the Great Reckoning was small in number. Experts did not expect the birth rate to rise very fast for some time. As with the plagues that went before, something cautious and dark had made a home in the human psyche. What did it know of new life, new beginnings? It ran the past over and over and asked, "Why would you bring life into this world?" Oh, to be sure, we'll forget again, but such things take time. It is good only the young can give birth.

A Light-Filled Abyss
Delana Sujhari

I hauled Vic up, even as he cringed away from me. "Dig a hole," I told Tebre. "Warren will check for a grave site; he always does."

She nodded. "And then?"

"Keep him occupied as long as you can...tell him I am asking for forgiveness from God and will return by evening."

"Forgiveness from God?" Vic laughed wildly.

I covered his mouth, leaning close to his ear. "You are going to get yourself killed," I said softly. "Now get hold of yourself."

Vic twisted away, his face a mask of rage. "You haven't seen what happens when you die, have you? You goddamn monk, all the shit you guys feed us. I should..."

Tebre grabbed Vic's throat and lifted him nearly off his feet. She glared at him as he kicked and gasped. "You're not dead anymore. But if even think of harming my friend, I will put you back where you were, make no mistake. I will hunt you myself."

"Tebre," I murmured, my hand on her arm. "Put him down." She released him at once then looked around the woods, her head cocked. I held my breath, trusting her keener senses.

"You need to go," she said.

I nodded, shoving Vic to get him started. "Where?"

I thought he would start in again. But his eyes cleared a little. I put a small GPS in his hands. "You have to lead, Vic. It's the only way."

His eyes were watering. His hands were shaking so bad I was afraid he would drop the piece of equipment. He kept blinking, trying to read the screen then finally indicated the direction with quick nod of his head. And we took off at a trot. I cast one look back at Tebre, and she half-raised her hand in farewell. There was a heartbeat when I wanted to call it all off. But then she was turning away, and I rushed to catch up with Vic.

We moved as fast as we could through the thick deadfall and vines. Vic stopped several times, adjusting our path. Each time we paused he seemed a bit calmer, but if I reached out to steady him, or tried to talk with him, he pulled away as if I was a monster.

But then, maybe I was.

I couldn't find a good rhythm in the woods; the terrain was too hilly, the footing and obstacles too unpredictable. Even long after our bodies were soaked with sweat, our hair plastered to our scalps, we pushed on. One hour turned to four, turned to six, and then darkness began to descend. My legs and lungs screamed.

"How much farther," I panted.

"Two hours. Maybe three," Vic answered, his voice sullen.

"We need to stop."

"I'm fine," he said, vaulting over a nearly waist-high fallen tree trunk.

"I'm not."

I leaned my hands on the mossy bark of a deadfall, my head sagging. If he had kept going at that moment, I wasn't sure I could have caught up with him. But he stopped after a few steps, and dropped to a crouch, his back against a tree trunk. "Some of the CoGs have good night vision," he said. "They're faster, too. We can't stay here."

I nodded, conserving my ragged breath.

We let the silence fall around us for a time.

Vic finally shifted, coming to his feet. His eyes were calmer now and the sweat had actually cleaned away the worst of the grime from his face. "There was supposed to be lights right?"

"What?" I asked.

"Lights. Or a celestial being. Or something."

I understood then, what he was asking. I couldn't meet his gaze. "I don't think anyone really knows what it is like to die," I said. "Not the Margas, not the scriptures, none of them."

"You want to know what I saw?" Vic asked. He put his hands on the tree trunk and looked me straight in the eye.

"I saw a storm of...of bits of sand. Or smaller than sand. But the sand was alive, and it razed me to the bone. It *loved* doing it." His face suddenly went soft, lost and lonely as a small boy can look. "No light, Ianto. Just things eating me from the inside out, and not being able to scream and then this awful blackness."

"I'm sorry," I said softly. I put all the compassion I could into it.

Vic pushed off the log, stepping back. "I thought you were just saying you were a CoG. You look so normal, you act decent. But whatever it is you did to me, something in you *likes* it. Something in you gets off on it," he said. "So I'm leading you back to the lodge, but don't think I don't see into you now. Don't touch me. And don't try to talk to me to make it OK."

If he had hit me, it wouldn't have taken my breath away as quickly as his words. I swallowed and nodded.

He put his back to me, and strode off again into the forest.

Chapter 34

The field trials have illustrated for us that sometimes the finest kind of control we can hope to achieve is like a scatter shot in poor light. Still, with so many Children of God, we'll hit something. We just need to point them in the correct general direction.

Nano-stim Field Trial Notes
Commander Leland

We belly-crawled the rest of the way, the lodge rising out of the night mist, its yellowed lights casting an aura around the building like an old painting. I heard laughter inside, and every so often a shadow moved past the window.

"How many staffers?" I whispered.

"I don't know; four or five maybe, if there are no new recruits," Vic answered. He wouldn't look at me. And I couldn't blame him. "What now?" he asked.

I edged away a bit, rolled onto my back and stared up at the lattice of branches overhead. The trees were rustling with the first breath of a wind from the ocean. I could feel them moving inside as well, the dance of moisture and light and rich soil.

"Ianto?" Vic snapped at me.

"I thought I'd know what to do when I got here," I said. "But all I want to do right now is walk away."

I could feel Vic's eyes on me, cold and hard. "You kill me and bring me back and now you want to just walk away."

I rolled my head, looking at his fierce young eyes. "Run away, actually. Keep running right into the ocean. Keep going out over my head. You understand? You ever felt that way, Vic?"

"Shut the fuck up, and do what you came here to do!" he hissed.

"I have already," I said quietly. I smiled at him sadly. "You're safe. Go on." I jerked my head toward the lodge, feeling the leaves crinkle beneath my skull. I sat up then, combing them out of my hair with my dirty fingers. "I'm tired, Vic. Time to for me to get out now. Tebre was right—I'm not God."

Vic looked toward the lodge and back at me, his eyes guarded and confused.

"It's OK," I said again. "Warren will track us here; he'll deal with whoever is in that lodge in his own unique way, so warn them all if that feels right to you. I don't want it on my hands, whatever either side decides to do. I'm going home." I eased myself a little further back from the lodge and stood slowly. Vic looked up at me from the ground. It was dark enough that I couldn't read his face, even with just this little distance between us. "Be well," I said, turning away.

Vic came off the ground so silently, I had almost no warning until I was sprawling on the forest floor with the breath knocked out of me. He snapped his arm around my throat, his legs scissoring around my waist. "Leland!" he screamed. "Get the fuck out here now!" His other fist slammed into my temple, twice in rapid succession. I jerked as blows hit my cheek, then the side of my nose. I could feel the cartilage give. I clawed at his grip, writhing with him, but couldn't get free, my breath choked off in my throat.

I couldn't kill him, though. Even right then, when it would have made sense to reach out and break him again, I couldn't do it. There was this tangled thought that I was supposed to be saving him, to seek atonement for killing him and throwing him into hell, only to drag him out again for my own purposes...to say sorry for the lives I had helped end, even when I thought my hands were clean.

My own selfish purposes, causing so much pain.

So I let him beat on me until the edges of my consciousness were ebbing, and the blows were from far away, something outside of me.

The other hands, when they came, were not much gentler. They dragged me to the edge of the woods, not particularly mindful what part of my body they had. I had only impressions of legs, and voices, and rough hands. Then I was face first on the gravel of the driveway, my hands wrenched up behind my back and thin plastic cutting into my wrists. I could have ripped through them, I suppose. Nothing would bind me again, not really. But I didn't.

I couldn't see through the blood haze, too stunned to even pull myself into a ball when someone kicked me hard in the ribs.

"They'll be right behind us," Vic said. "This bastard is one of them, you believe it?"

"Vic, isn't it? We thought you were dead with your squad. Are they hard on your trail, kid?"

I knew that voice, so calm. I remembered dinner conversations with him, not so very long ago, when I was locked away from the world. Leland. And he was the very answer I did not want to know: Spirit Marga was somehow involved with the squads sent to hunt the Children of God.

"They can't be that far behind," Vic said. "You gonna plug this one or not?"

Someone rolled me to my back, and the gravel ground into my bare hands and wrists. I tried to look up through my broken face, but everything was a play of light and shadow and red haze.

"Oh, my God," Leland muttered. "Everybody back inside. Now! Break out the arms and contact our field man for immediate forest withdrawal. NOW, I said!"

I could feel him standing by me, even after the others had raced away to carry out his orders, half-dragging Vic with them. "God, what a mess," he said under his breath. "What the fuck are you doing here, Ianto? You're supposed to be with Warren."

I could tell by his voice he didn't expect me to reply, but Warren's name jerked at me. How did Leland know Warren? Or had I even heard right?

"High Priestess Cyntia is going to execute me for this," he muttered. "God damn it, Ianto! You are the most stubborn, unpredictable...." He stopped, and I could hear him listening. He crouched then and grabbed my face painfully, turning it toward him. "I know you can kill me right now, and I have no idea why you haven't except maybe you're too fucked up to get a bead on me. Now you listen and you listen to me good. I know you think Spirit Marga is hunting the Children of God, but that's not what this is about. This has been a test, Ianto. Warren was supposed to bring you back in. Just a few more weeks of observation was all the head of the Spirit Marga wanted. Just a few more weeks. We needed to see what you would do in the field. We're just playing parts here, understand? And it's mostly over now."

"No," I whispered. "Too many dead."

"It's not what you think. And I don't have the time to explain it to you right now, not all the details." He shook his head, a shadow to my swelling eyelids. "It wasn't supposed to go down quite like this, you understand? I need you to tell me you won't kill my men in there, you get it? The data had to be pure. And none of this is their fault."

I looked right through him, and then shut my eyes.

"Ianto? Can you hear me?" Leland shook me hard.

"Break my neck, Leland. Snap it. Call it an accident." I said through my swollen lips. "Because if you don't do that, I can't promise you a damn thing."

Leland went quiet for a moment. And then something harder than a fist hit me and everything went dark.

Chapter 35

Citizens, in general, only picture the Spirit Marga Temple complex or the vast Mansion of the Science Marga when asked about the geography of these two great powers. But these are tiny and insignificant dots on the larger map of the territory and infrastructure actually held by the Margas. Oh, to be sure, they have not divided up the entire world between them, but their presence throughout the world is much more vast and subtle than most people realize.

Geography of the Margas
Ronnie Calhan

After my beating, I woke in a bed, the first one I had slept in for months. The sheets smelled a little of wood smoke. I had the shadowy impression of huge beams overhead; my vision was blurry. The window had been boarded shut from the inside, but light still seeped through the cracks, light I saw as something shimmering and almost alive. I tried to sit, but my head spun so badly that I immediately lay back down on the pillow and closed my eyes.

A hand touched my forehead, then my cheek, and I could feel the tickling, crackling energy of a Binder. I tried turning my head, moving more slowly this time. The healer gently held my shoulders down. "Please don't move, Ianto. I'm not done here."

The voice was deep and calm in a way I had never heard before.

"Warren," I whispered.

"Yes," he said quietly. "Now lie still."

I felt my heart rate pick up and clenching my jaw, I turned and looked at him. It took a while for my eyes to focus, to look up at his dark, slanted eyes and long, loose hair. All the features were right, but the kind and concerned expression was out of character for him. He was clothed in a brilliant red habit, a small insignia I didn't recognize set at his left shoulder. Red was the color of the Spirit Marga's healing corp. It made no sense.

I licked my too-dry lips. "What's going on?" My speech was slurred, my mouth and cheek still swollen.

"I'm trying to fix you up. I think the drugs they gave you are interfering a little, that, and

220

Tebre is still debriefing with Leland. When she gets here, the two of us in tandem should have you feeling better."

I closed my eyes. Aside from the headache, my body didn't hurt, but I was so disoriented that I could feel my stomach rolling. "Not the right answer," I murmured.

Warren sighed. "I know. But I'm not cleared to answer the other questions you have."

I rolled my head toward him. "Not a blooded Binder."

Warren understood my question at once. "Actually, I am blooded as you say but I am not the monster you expected me to be. It's been a pretty distasteful few months for me, too, Ianto. At least what I can remember of them." His hands moved on my face again, and I made a feeble attempt to push them away.

"Stop." But my voice was weak. "Drugs?"

"Yes, I do believe Leland ordered synaptic inhibitors, meant to confuse the signals between your nervous system and your nanotech. Experimental stuff."

"Why?"

"Because you told Leland to break your neck or you would make him regret it. Or something like that."

"Still no promises."

"And that's why you're drugged. Are you feeling much pain now?"

"Head hurts, nothing else," I said. The words wanted to come out backward, but I reordered them carefully before speaking. "Might throw up."

"I've got a bowl here, just in case. Let me know."

I heard a door open. "Can I come in?" Tebre's voice was strained and tired. I tried to roll my head toward her, and immediately felt my stomach's contents rise into my throat. The bowl was under my chin in an instant, the two Binders cradling me until there was simply nothing left to throw up.

"Why is he so sick?" Tebre asked. She knelt on the floor and her hand on my brow was cool. "The injuries themselves are largely healed." I tried to look at her face, but couldn't focus. My stomach rolled again, and I could feel myself break out in a cold, clammy sweat. And then, I was sinking back, the way a wave oozes back from the seashore.

"They've blanketed his nanotech with a drug but it's like I can't get the life force within him to come back up." Warren said. "Something is interfering. I can't make the connection with his energy and tissues like I usually can. It has to be the drug; I've never experienced this before with other patients. It's like the drug hasn't just affected the interaction between his body and the technology. It's like his whole system is shutting down."

I tried to follow their conversation, but huge parts of me were floating away. I could dimly feel Tebre rest a hand on my heart and one on my stomach. Her touch felt very far off now. "He's pulling back, Warren." I could hear her voice was filled with concern, but the words took me long moments to translate.

"Pulling back," he echoed. "Yes. That's a good description."

"I've felt this with animals before they die; everything pulls down and in. That's happening to Ianto."

I heard her words, but they were not making sense. Dying? Was she saying I was dying? Was this, the slow receding of vision and sound and senses, the prelude to death? If so, it was not the terrible experience Vic had had. This was peaceful, a slow drowning in softness.

"You have to heal with the blood, Warren," Tebre finally said. "From the inside, maybe you can help. Detox him. Clean his system of the drug, if that is what is causing this. Or find what is."

I forced my eyes back open. "No," I said weakly. I'm not sure if I actually made any sound, my breath seemed so far away.

Warren put his hand along the edge of my face, looking me in the eye. His eyebrows were drawn together over his nose and I could see the pain in him. "I hate doing it, Ianto. The blood lust is real, more real each time I do it. But I'm in control. I'm a monk of the Spirit Marga like yourself, and not a monster. Tebre is right; it is the best way." He looked up at her. "Go get Leland. Tell him we need a possible way to flush this medication if I am not successful. Hurry."

I heard Tebre push herself back from my bed, and head toward the door. Warren put a hand on my chest and the other on my forehead. I tried to get my muscles to obey me, to push him away, but everything felt too heavy. "Still, Ianto. Please. You must be still." And then he tipped my head to the side, his lips dipping to my throat. I sucked in my breath as his sharp teeth cut through my skin. The pain lasted only a moment before the injury he had inflicted went cool and numb.

It was actually an interesting sensation, to sense the presence of another within me. I could feel him spread through my body, as fast as my blood stream could carry him. Part of me wanted to fight, but part of me wanted to dance with the new presence, with the energy swirling down into my bones and out to the tips of my fingers. I felt as if tiny parts of myself collided again and again with him, resistant and at the same time pleading for help, as if he had become a light in the gathering darkness and stillness of my body.

And in that darkness, bonds were forged as if small pieces of myself and small pieces of Warren attached themselves to each other. I could feel changes happening, the trajectory of my slow descent being altered, and a wild ecstasy building with it, such brilliance, as if every blood vessel was exploding with light. And parts of myself ripped through the drugged bindings and I flooded back into Warren, feeling his heart, the play of electrical arcs in his brain, the heightened senses of the Binder, the physical power of his muscles. As magnificent and as breakable as any other form I had ever touched. I laughed out loud with the pure exhilaration of it all.

Warren threw himself backwards, stumbling and sprawling. His eyes were wide, the pupils dilated. I could still see my own blood on his lips where he had not wiped it away.

I sat up slowly as he came to his feet in a rush and dropped into a defensive crouch. There was a heartbeat of a moment when I would have gone to him, would have torn into him to feel that ecstasy again, the dance of light and raw power. Indeed, it would not take such a physical act; I was within him as much as he was within me. But I saw the terror, then, in his eyes; the look of a blooded Binder terrified of *me*. And I sank back into myself, willing my muscles to loosen. I could hear his breath, so ragged as he watched me.

I felt the wildness slowly wash away, and I felt only a rising fatigue and aching loneliness.

"What are you, Ianto?" Warren asked. He half-crouched on the floor, as if I would spring from the bed at him.

"I don't know anymore," I answered, turning my face away.

Chapter 36

We religious think our minds are the key to discipline, discernment, even compassion. In this age we have forgotten the wily Fates, explained away the wrath of God, laughed at the idea of Shaitan. In the end, it will not be our minds that truly misled us; rather, it will be those ancient memories come back to life and once more given life.

When this Veil Falls
Bishop Vorha

I rested my hand on the green habit that lay folded on my lap and stared into the room's twilight. The clouds had descended again, and a light rain tapped on the roof. I had become so used to the rain during my months in the forest that to hear it muffled and far away seemed to me a great sadness, a part of myself cut off.

They had left me alone for the better part of the day after my shared experience with Warren. I still had no answers, and was not sure I wanted them. I didn't sense anything in particular keeping me here, in the room or even in the lodge. Yet still I sat, hand on the fabric of my past.

"You told me to help them," I murmured. "I trusted that. But it has all been som kind of lie."

"I only knew what I could see through your eyes." I stopped myself from jerking my head toward the sound, and the shadowy form moved from behind me to the wooden walls. He rested his hands on his hips as he walked along the great timbers, tipping his head up to study the ceiling. "This is like the great halls the Northmen build." I looked up at him carefully, this spirit who haunted me.

"I'm glad we can speak now, like in the woods. Who are you?" I asked.

He turned to look at me then. "A friend, it would seem."

I shook my head. "And you can't tell me what is happening here, to me?"

"Can you see the Wareffa pack that I have hunted for a week?" the elf asked in return. "What should I do about them?"

"I don't know what you are talking about."

"I could show you, and you still would not understand," he said. It was not said with malice, merely with a sad sense of loneliness and practicality. "We each see only glimpses into these parallel worlds. If I guided you wrong it was because you drew me to you and the answer I gave was the one you were seeking. It helped you survive. As you have done for me." He glanced back at the habit on my lap. "Yours?"

I nodded, silently.

"Will you put it back on?" he asked.

"I don't know." I put the palm of my hand to my head, leaning on the chair arm. "I'm frightened. More frightened than all that time I spent in the woods. More frightened than when I have been ready to die."

The elf moved toward me, and then hunkered so we were eye to eye. His face was still so shadowy, shifting, like watching someone through several blowing veils. "Dying is easy," he said.

I hated the knowledge ringing in his voice, even as I took comfort in it.

"If you are frightened, you must simply play this thing through like a game. Dance with it. Because when you master that, there will be no fear." He rose and kissed my forehead.

No fear.

I raised my eyes to him, but the vision was gone.

Chapter 37

I am not sure at what point we began to understand that we needed a shield rather than weapon to resist the incursion of the Game into our reality. I suppose once we accepted that Nuress was a living creature, we were left with all sorts of moral questions, not the least of which was what right do we have to end her life? She is, in fact, someone's child whether they claim her or not. I think that is why Ianto's mother fled the Margas—as a high-level tech, she could see the threat Nuress posed, but could no more destroy the AI than she could her own unborn son. However, it seems she had no compunction at all about giving Ianto a set of skills (and hence a set of difficult choices) to use against the Game. In the end, if history views us as cowards, it was because we took too seriously the old adage: "If a mother loves her own child more than any other, there will be war."

The Metal Cloud of Consciousness
High Priestess Cyntia Molair

I studied myself in the mirror. My face was still drawn, my eyes underlined with dark smudges of fatigue. My hair had grown longer in the woods; it brushed just below my shoulders in a tangle of unruly brown curls. The green softness of the habit at least felt familiar and comforting. I glanced down at the hood in my hands, weighing it carefully then set it aside. There would come a time, perhaps, when I would need its safety. But today, I needed to see and be seen.

Fearless.

Tebre shifted on the bed where she perched. She still wore jeans, topped with a warm woolen sweater knitted in blacks and reds. I glanced at her and smiled. "I'm ready."

As the days passed, I learned that Tebre had been a lucky accidental meeting in the woods. That she stayed here, with Warren and Leland and myself only surprised me a little. And I knew she had seen the truth in Warren, even when I could not. To see her belief vindicated must have felt good to her. It simply made me uneasy.

She stood, her towering height dwarfing me. "All the Children of God are dressed in their habits and the main living room of the lodge has become some kind of chapel now." She looked at me uncertainly. "Are you sure I can attend? I am not Spirit Marga."

I nodded, hoping my gaze reassured her. "You are a part of what happened in the forest. You saved my life, and you deserve to hear the explanation."

She brushed at my hair, sweeping it back over my shoulder. "You are frightened," she said.

"Because I don't know what we will hear. I don't know if more will be expected of us. I don't know if I will be sent away and never see you again." I touched her arm. "You are a friend, Tebre, one of my very few."

"That will not change," she said.

I held her gaze, hoping my eyes would say all I could not. "Time to go."

I let her lead through the door of my suite, and down the hallway toward the lodge living room. The low ceilings that forced Tebre to gently lower her head opened up into a lovely two-story room with floor to ceiling windows. Such light! The space glowed with the rich honey color of the wood walls and floors.

The members of the assembled Spirit Marga had begun to take their seats on cushions in neat rows. Many habit colors were here, the green of the hermits and land-workers, the blue of the priests, the red of the healers, the deep purple of the teachers, the black of the musicians and writers, a rainbow of colors. I took in their races -- Weres, with their great shaggy head and tapered snouts, the Seafarin, with their wide and unblinking eyes, the Shodo so small and delicate, with gentle wings folded against their specially cut habits. The Binder, Warren, blazing and tall in his red habit lifted a hand toward Tebre but would not meet my eye. He motioned to a cushion beside him.

"Go," I said quietly to Tebre. "He needs you."

She took my hand quickly then released it with a squeeze and threaded her way through the long lines of cushions to join him. I sat far back, settling with a small rock of my spine into my cross-legged position, hands neatly folded on my lap.

Nobody sat near me.

At the front of our space, where two great windows came together like the prow of a ship, a single chair sat empty. Off to its side, a lone cushion perched on its larger padded square. Moments later, Leland entered, and eased himself onto the cushion, head bowed a little toward his chest as he settled there. I dropped my gaze, not meeting his eye, although I could feel him seek me out with his own.

For nearly half an hour, we waited.

And then, the Children of God came almost silently to their feet. I followed more slowly, turning slightly to see who would come to take the simple chair. My breath caught then.

I was not expecting to see Jean.

She entered with a measured step, her hair bound up and severe at the nape of her neck. Her deep blue habit seemed to drain her face of its color, leaving her brown eyes two dark smudges on her skin. Leland bowed to her, and all bowed with him, except me. I stood stiffly, gathering a handful of my habit's fabric in my left hand as if that could keep me rooted.

She turned to face the people of the Spirit Marga and held her hands over them in prayer. "In exchange for those lost and injured, we have gained in knowledge. For those heartbroken and alone, we have come together in solidarity. For those lives we have taken, we stand absolved in the face of the greater Divine and Good."

"Ameyn," the children of God answered, bowing again. But I stood unbent, my eyes on Jean's face. She looked at me quickly, then away, her face still pale and schooled.

Jean took her seat, and all followed her example. With her hands folded on her lap, she gazed out on each face. "It has been a hard few months. The trials we have just finished, the ones that we run here every three years, have had results we must all find disquieting. As most of you know, in the first years of the trials, we could find very few who would willingly hurt the Children of God. And then, the numbers began to grow. And this trial, we had more people come forward than we had space for hunters."

I tried to process what she was saying, tried fitting the pieces together.

"The trials help us glean from the population any people, including other Children of God, who would willingly hunt and kill those not like themselves. We remove them from the population and also monitor the tenor of the larger civilization for signs of unrest."

Jean lowered her voice. "It is a brutal technique, some would say, but it has been effective. As the analysis comes in, I will be sure to meet with each of you to discuss your own roles in the trials this year. Please know that your contributions have helped protect the many Children of God all over the world. We will continue to find ways to educate and monitor the general population for further signs of unrest."

I stood then. "And the mutilated bodies we found in the forest?"

Jean raised her chin. "I did not ask for questions."

Tebre rose, her height only accentuated by the low seats. "Answer him. He speaks for me as well."

Jean turned her head slowly toward Tebre, and finally I could see a hint of color in her cheeks. "Those were plants. Bodies of those who died from natural causes."

"Why do it?" I asked.

Jean glanced at me, then back to Tebre. "Each of the Spirit Marga monks around you, those involved with the trial, were fitted with sensitive psycho-sensory equipment that helped us gage their responses. The trial is not just about the genetically human hunters, it is about how the Children of God handle their own responses to death, military tactics, leadership and the like."

"I didn't feel any of the equipment."

"Which was also part of the test," she said, again leveling her gaze at me.

"Why would you need that data?" I asked.

Jean shook her head. "Please be seated, Ianto, Tebre. When we meet one on one we can discuss this further."

"I look forward to our conversation, then." I gave her a half-bow, and turned to leave. Out of the corner of my eye, I saw Tebre begin to come after me, but Warren's hand at her elbow stopped her. Just as well.

I could feel the eyes on me, as the Children of God considered my words and actions. But no one else followed me.

I opened the door to the outside, and stepped onto a wide porch that ran the entire side and back of the lodge. I trembled there, in a wash of anxiety. Breathing slowly, I opened myself up to the forest. The trees stood tall and still, their feet in black shadows shaded with a froth of green. I closed my eyes and let my mind stray into the forest, feeling the roots and sharp dry tips of the pines. I touched the edges of a bird's consciousness, felt its heart fluttering in its chest.

And then, I felt something else entirely.

I opened my eyes, frowning, and followed the porch railing around the corner of the house. I drew up short, then, my eyes resting on a shrouded pile stacked neatly against the wall of the lodge. I didn't have to twitch the white canvas away; the red stains and regular lumps told me enough. I counted at least five bodies there. I knelt and rested my hand on the cold surface and sent them a quick and bitter prayer.

But the feeling, the sensation persisted, an apprehension of a slow, disjointed heartbeat. I moved down the steps across the gravel and into the woods. There was a fairly well-worn path, and I took it, meandering past two great cedars. The sensation of the struggling heartbeat grew stronger, and I moved faster in the underbrush, despite the drag of my habit.

I scrambled over a fallen log, landing softly on the dirt. It was only when I looked up that I stumbled. A man dangled from a sturdy tree branch, his feet barely touching the ground. His head had slumped forward against his naked chest. Long rivulets of crusted blood had coursed from his wrists to his armpits.

I went to him then, my eyes scanning how to cut him down. I put up a hand, feeling into the fibers that bound him, and the ropes began to fray and give way. I half-caught the man as he dropped, but his weight pulled me to the ground with him. I rolled him off me, settling him as best as I could in the leaves and needles. I turned his face toward me then suddenly felt sick. Though his face was deeply bruised and lacerated, I recognized Vic immediately.

"Oh, God," I whispered. I cupped the edge of his face with my hand. "Who did this to you?"

"In a way, you did."

I whipped around to find Warren watching me, his red habit open at his neck.

"When you made him bring you back here, you ensured this would happen," he said. He hopped effortlessly over the downed tree even as I came to my feet.

"You tortured him? For what possible reason?" I asked.

"I didn't do it," Warren answered. He stalked to the other side of Vic's unconscious form. "He should be dead. He has lasted longer than the others." Warren glanced at Ianto." He beat you almost as badly," he said. "So put him out of his misery. Turn him off and come back up to the lodge. Let's be done with this."

"Done with all this?" I cried. "I'll never be done with all this!"

I dropped back to Vic's side. "Help me." I looked up into Warren red eyes. "Stop playing this damn game, Warren. Help me!"

The Binder didn't move.

I lifted Vic's lacerated wrists and shutting my eyes, kissed the torn flesh. I felt myself flooding into him, just as I had with Warren. But I fought with the parts of myself that wanted to destroy and the part of me that could seek out and heal. Through half-open eyes, I could see the wound knit itself shut. But I couldn't reach deeper. I put my hand on Vic's heart, feeling inside and out the trembling weakness of it. "Come on, come on," I whispered.

And then, Warren was kneeling on the other side of him, a wicked dagger with a toothed edge in his hand. I froze, my eyes on the weapon, but unable to move. Warren looked at me for a moment then slammed the knife into the soft soil by Vic's head. He reached out and his long fingers covered my own. For a moment we held each other's eyes, and then he nodded. As Tebre had taught me, I dropped my chin toward my chest and opened myself up to Warren's guidance. The energy in him pressed back the furious, hungry energy in myself and I could feel us healing Vic together.

But when the time came, bits of me wouldn't withdraw. I struggled, feeling him too much now, the suction of his veins, the increasing flashes of consciousness. "Warren..." I gasped. "I can't..."

I felt the big Binder hands close on my shoulders, and rip me away. I spun into the mud, one hand splayed to hold my face up. For one moment I was sure I would retch, and I forced myself to breathe through my nose, low and even.

Beside me, Vic gasped and rolled to his side, then staggered to his feet. He stumbled back from us both and fell hard. His eyes were wide, panic stricken.

I pressed myself up, staggered a few feet and reached down to pull the knife out of the soft ground. He shoved himself back with his feet, his breath coming in fast, panicking gulps. I extended a palm toward him, trying to calm him. Warren hovered behind me, still kneeling, a low growl welled up deep in his chest like a warning.

I edge forward another step and knelt just out of reach. Trembling, I laid the blade carefully on my open palms and extended it toward him. "Take it, Vic."

He shook his head wildly, not understanding.

Warren stood slowly, his form a dark shadow rising.

I glanced back at Warren, and shook my head. Then I drove the knife into the ground between Vic and myself, and put a palm on each leg. I bowed my head, my eyes cast down.

No fear.

Vic lunged then, snatching the dagger up. He grasped my hair, jerking my head to one side. I closed my eyes, unmoving, even when I could feel the blade scoring my skin. I could feel the blood lust and panic in him, the fast calculations of adrenaline-fired nerves, and then the racking trembles as his conscious mind struggled to catch up to his body.

I could hear Warren's footsteps behind me, then the soft crunch as he, too, knelt.

I could feel the blade tremble in his hands. Vic pulled the knife away from my throat.

"Go," I said softly. "For god's sake, go, Vic."

Without a word, he turned and stumbled his way into the forest.

Warren and I sat unmoving, on our knees long after Vic had gone. I don't know if the Binder found a kind of absolution in our gesture. I only know I was left with an even deeper sense of confusion and something shading toward fury.

Chapter 38

In the Upanishads it is written that we must cry out, demand to be led from unreality to Reality, from darkness to Light, to an understanding of our own immortality. Such knowledge has to be wrung out, experienced. Only then can we say, "Ah, yes. Of course. It has always been so. And Amen."

Drunken Days
High Priestess Cyntia Molair

Warren finally stood, and came around in front of me. He bent down, offering his hand, and I took it, allowing him to half-drag me to my feet. I shook with fatigue and the creeping cold of the damp woods. Fog was rolling in, rising as if the ground itself burned.

"You actually enjoy tempting death, don't you?" he asked.

I ignored him, my eyes on the deep forest. "What stories will he take back, I wonder? And who will listen to him?" I looked up at Warren's long, thin face for a long moment. "Thank you," I said at last.

"No need. Your act healed a part of myself," he murmured. "Tell me, why did you think to kneel? How did you know he wouldn't kill you?"

"I didn't," I replied. "I just trusted. I suppose I was trying to find my own kind of absolution, the kind the Marga could never give. But it doesn't feel like I am done with it yet."

"God must love you," Warren said. He smiled just a little. "Which is to say, I'm sorry for you."

"'Woe to those who God loves, for them waits the cross and the syringe, the bottle and the public's cold eye,' Book of Tethla, Chapter 17." I looked down at Vic's blood on my hands.

"But then, the weaver will have her way, pulling his bare ligaments through warps of fire and in wonder shall he rule," Warren answered. "I like happy endings." He smiled wide, his dark teeth like pointed shadows.

It was my turn to give him a cautious chuckle, and then I turned my eyes from his again. "I'm not sure I believe in those anymore."

"In what?"

"Happy endings."

Warren cocked his head at me. "That only means you aren't a child anymore." He rested his hand on my shoulder for a moment. "We need to head back, Ianto."

"They'll go after him, won't they?" I asked quietly, looking at the way Vic had gone.

"Not me," Warren said with a shrug. "But yes. Only if he is very lucky will he make it out of the woods. Unless they want him to make it out, I suppose. But then, he has a good head start after all. We shall see." He beckoned to me and started walking. I dropped in behind him, slower and more awkward. Some things did not change.

"Why did you do it, all those months of killing?"

Warren glanced over his shoulder. "Why did you?"

"I didn't kill, not after that first time the hunters shot me," I said.

"You made it so they could be killed," he countered. "There is no difference there, except that the blame could be laid on others."

"I didn't want our Children of God to die," I said. "We weren't armed like they were. I leveled the playing field. And I wasn't trying to avoid blame. I was trying to keep you all alive."

"Except in the past, we have been able to claim guns with our victories, and thus even the odds ourselves. But you broke the guns. You kept us helpless. But you would not kill them for us. You worked both sides against each other." I caught the shadow of reproach in his voice.

"Working guns would have come at a greater cost," I countered, ignoring the rest of his statement. "Besides, when I was shot, there were Children of God with the hunting party."

"That happens sometimes. Not all of us are as pure as you." This time the mocking sound was anything but faint. "Some can be bought," Warren returned.

"You haven't answered my question, Warren. Why do it all in the first place if you knew the ruse, if you knew you weren't fighting for your life? How could that sick game reveal anything about us or the normal humans that other studies couldn't have shown?" I halted, a little breathless. "Warren. Stop. Answer me."

Warren turned toward me, and put his hand against one great cedar tree to his right. "This Marga is the only family I have," he said. He let the words hang there for a moment. "I was turned out of my home when I was eleven. My parents were terrified of me. During the Great Reckoning, in the streets of the city, bodies were piled waiting for the cremation trucks to take them away. Older boys, unchanged, ran in the streets and beat those of us without parents or protection. I was lucky; I was big and I healed quickly when a rock or bottle found its mark. And as I grew, I became fast as well, which meant I could avoid or disarm the humans. Most of the street children were not so lucky. In time, it was on the streets where I learned that I could also heal others. And lead them."

He looked at me then. "The stories you have heard all your life, Ianto, that there is peace between the Children of God and the humans have always been lies, at least in the city I came from. The Margas did manage to take back some control, though, and the Emperium stepped up patrols and care centers and in the end, I was invited to join the healing arm of the Spirit Marga. I was fed. I was clothed and educated. And for a while, after the chaos of the Great Reckoning, I thought perhaps we had won the humans over. But the trials show that the fury is still brewing, and not just in the humans. It will erupt again at some point. The Children of God must understand how to fight and survive. How to work together, to be a single people."

"So we can go to war against our own kind?" I asked bitterly. "We are still human, at our cores, Warren."

He cocked his head, his eyes suddenly sharp and raptor-like. "You may pass as one of them, but the Sea Children? The Were's? We Binders? Come, Ianto. We are *not* human. That is why they call us the Children of God; how can we be more blessed or cursed than that?" He drew in a breath through his nose. "No, we help control the more violent of the humans by taking them out of the population. We learn important skills in the field. And my family has promised us a singular honor. The Spirit Marga has told some of us that one day, Ianto, we will be the ones who they will send off this planet into the stars. We will take the great books and practices out there, spreading like seeds on the wind. Not the humans, whose time of power and glory are winding down into the dust."

I took a step toward him. "Into dust? What do you mean?"

"The stars, Ianto. We will be the ones to go, to leave this planet for the humans. We train to survive because one day we will be asked to step out on alien soil and make a new home for ourselves. We do not belong here. We never have. We will go, one day. And so I do as I am told; I kill when I am meant to be a healer. I learned the blood way and will always burn with it. But I will have a home that is mine one day, and this family of the Spirit Marga is the vessel that will see me to it."

I nodded, and started walking again, this time, Warren dropping in behind me.

"You are quiet," he said.

"I just wonder," I said quietly. "Why I have never heard of all this before. And I wonder if Jean meant to leave me in the path of those hunters now. What did she expect me to do or learn? Were you told to find me?"

Warren was silent behind me.

I stopped again, turning to face him. "You were. I did hear Leland right. You were expecting me."

"Your life has never been your own, Ianto." The look of pity he gave me shook me inside. "It will never be your own. I think they only ponder if you are best used as a weapon or..." He shook his head.

"Or what, Warren?" I stepped up to him, fists clenched so hard my knuckles ached. "Or what?"

"I have heard you called several things...a mind, a weapon and a wall."

"A wall?" I echoed.

"Does it make any sense to you?" Warren asked, his head tipping with genuine curiosity, as if he chose not to read the anger in my body language.

"No." With that, the fury dissipated again. I sat down on a mossy stump and sank my head into my hands. "How can I go back?" I asked. "You talk of family; I'm alone, Warren." I looked up at him. "Each time I kill, it's easier. Vic said there is something in me that enjoys it. And when you healed me..."

Warren stiffened, looking away.

"What frightened you so much then?" I asked the question with my voice pitched low. "Because you *were* frightened, just a few days ago." I looked up at him, seeing his revulsion. "Warren. Please. What did you feel?"

Warren drew in a long breath then met my eye again. "A blooded binder feels the lust, the holding in the hand of life and death. The moment is brilliant with ecstasy and longing and raw power. We become that which we heal by the blood, possess them, become something larger, stronger. And then it fades, and we die our own small death of withdrawal, as with any drug. That weakness and loneliness can press us to hurt and heal again and again. But in the end, we are never more than we were when we began. Indeed, we may be much less." He swallowed, and I noticed how he struggled to hold my gaze. "You, Ianto, when I entered you in the healing way, you flooded back into me a hundred times more powerful than myself. I was the one taken, I was the one consumed. I did not heal you. You took the healing power from me and healed yourself. You hold it still; a part of me ripped away and bound with you. You didn't feel it?"

I dropped my eyes away so he couldn't read the recognition there. An image of the little girl from my past flitted through my brain. "Perhaps. I'm sorry. I don't know how or why that happened. But as you could see, I couldn't heal Vic by myself."

"Because Vic was not invading you," Warren said quietly.

"I didn't hurt Tebre when she healed me months ago."

"She did not use the blood way. And perhaps you did not see Tebre as an enemy," he suggested slowly. "But I..."

I nodded then. "Perhaps part of me were still seeing the Warren I thought I knew from the woods."

"I think you would have killed me," he said quietly. "No. That's not quite right. Not killed, but taken me into yourself. But the balance of your fear, the drugs in your system, your own mind putting the pieces together...somehow, you decided to break that link. I saw enough, though. You are terrifying."

"And yet, you followed me out here to bring me back," I said suddenly.

He nodded, his red eyes flickering.

"If I don't go?" Before he could answer, I held up my hand, silencing him. "God's beloved," I murmured. "Of course, I'll go back." I looked up at him and smiled sadly. "I hope, at the end of all of this, I do get to meet the Weaver face to face. She will have a lot of explaining to do."

Warren tipped his head. "One day," he answered, "she will have a great deal of explaining to do to us all."

Chapter 39

We are a very uneven society, technologically speaking. We can broadcast holo-images, but it took years to figure out the new virus that cut our world population by more than half. We are fairly proficient at nanotech-assisted surgeries, but our energy sources are still staggeringly expensive. Our food production is finally globally adequate, but the nutrition content falls off every year, requiring more and more supplementation. We suppose that many great minds died during the plagues, or that the resulting chaos in our urban centers retarded certain areas of research. Sometimes, however, the gaps in our technology seem most surgical in their precision. It is like someone or something wants to hobble us.

Technology's Shadow
Gaulus Piers

Warren and I walked into the lodge to find it empty. The living room cushions had been restacked, all the lights switched off. Warren ducked outside and returned moments later. "One transport left. Do we wait?"

A movement in the hall drew both of our attentions. I had half expected Jean or Leland, but the small elderly woman who stood there unbowed and regal brought Warren to his knees at once. He dropped his head, eyes cast down. "High Priestess Cyntia," he said. The reverence in him was so palpable that I had to fight the urge not to join him on his knees before her. Instead, I offered her only the slightest bow of my head.

I knew her from image and speeches, rumors and tales. But I had never shared space with her before, the head of the entire Spirit Marga.

Her pale eyes held me for a moment then looked back at Warren. "I assume you have good reason for leaving the briefing today?"

Warren glanced at me sideways, and Cyntia sighed. "Ianto. Why does that not surprise me?"

I startled at my name, blinking stupidly at her.

One wrinkled hand gestured for Warren to stand. "Wait for us outside, Healer."

He climbed to his feet, hesitating. She fixed him with the hard stare of a leader used to being obeyed. "Now."

"It's all right, Warren," I said. I didn't take my eyes from Cyntia, but I followed Warren's retreat with my ears. The priestess narrowed her eyes a little at me, very aware I had overstepped my authority when I spoke. I met her eyes, my chin lifting.

Something in her gave then, and she walked slowly past me, to the vacant chair under the soaring windows.

"You'll excuse me if I sit? I am not a young woman anymore." She eased herself down carefully, but still with a certain amount of grace. I could, in that moment, imagine her about Jean's age, and what a force of will and physical beauty she must have commanded. She laid her hands neatly on her lap, and for a long moment we looked at each other. Finally, she seemed satisfied and gestured for me to come closer. I moved with no great hurry, a few steps only, and then stood at a kind of attention with my arms at my sides.

She smiled a little to herself. "So now you will tell me, why did the Spirit Marga allow their own to kill and be killed?"

I tipped my head with a small shake. "Excuse me, High Priestess?"

"Your analysis. Speak it."

"Warren explained what he could," I began quietly.

"Warren knows nothing," she said softly.

My stomach tightened. "Then you should perhaps enlighten me, High Priestess." My words came out clipped and tight. I didn't want to give the power back to her, but there seemed no other choice. Because frankly, beneath her gaze, battered by the months, I was pathologically curious in a dark and fearful kind of way.

She held me with her sharp eyes. "Your arrogance is not as appealing as you think, Ianto." She settled a bit deeper into the chair. "Let's see if your mind is a bit more worth my time. In a matter of days, Warren shifted from a blooded binder to your healer to someone you are beginning to trust. Does that not seem odd to you?"

I frowned. "He was playing a role that this Marga set him to. You own him, you know. Body and soul. Complete devotion. And when he was released from that role, I began to see the real man. Tebre could always see it. I understand why he feels different to me now. He is no longer acting a part."

"Like Warren, *you* understand nothing," she replied.

I held my tongue, though a sharp comeback hovered there in my throat.

"What if I told you we have perfected a way to suggest actions to the Children of God?" she said.

"Suggest?" I returned her own words to her, my eyes asking her to clarify.

"It's not perfect yet," she said. "But we are making progress, with the help of the Science Marga of course. It is a disquieting progress, though. Shifting hormonal balances, adrenal stimulation, suppressing some higher brain functions sporadically. We don't control them in the proper sense of the word. But we have learned we can influence them and their subsequent behavior. And if we can do this, then so can others."

I had gone cold inside. "Then the story Warren believes..."

"Oh, true enough in its bits and pieces. There is a growing unrest between the Children of God and the human population but not to the level that Warren believes. Tell me, Ianto, doesn't it seem strange to you that our own monks would willingly walk into a woods for months, fight and kill simply to retrieve data? Ludicrous. Their whole lives have been devoted to study, to peace, to healing. But with the smallest alterations through the nanotech in their bodies, they can be pushed to be something other than they are. As you were pushed."

I looked away from her then. I couldn't quite control the tremor of rage in my body. And when I looked back at her face, she nodded. "It's subtle, no? Righteous anger, play to your pride, cultivate your somewhat innate wish to care for others. Yet, I must say, aside from the first initial murders, you fought us rather admirably whether you knew it or not. Burying the dead, disabling arms instead of out and out killing the genetic humans. And then, convincing that convict to bring you back to the lodge..."

"Vic was just a kid."

"No, Ianto. Vic was young, but the word kid implies an innocence he did not possess. None of the men and women sent against you would have lived out the year anyway. They were taken from prison, had mild memory implants that suggested to them that they had volunteered for the hunt. Your young Vic has been convicted of at least three murders, two of which were Children of God."

"Lies within lies," I said bitterly.

"My daughter has tried on numerous occasions to talk to you about a purpose for your life, Ianto. You are unique among the Children of God. There is not one other person who can send and re-home their nanotech, who is fairly resistant to outside suggestions, and frankly who can kill so cleanly, even, we suspect, surgically. We would like to begin to teach you how better to use your skills. Hone them."

"To what purpose?" I said quietly. "If you can influence the Children of God, then they can kill for you. Or break things. If you have control of them, of what real use am I? I am just one, High Priestess. And I would not be cooperative by choice. My experiences over this year, experiences you have admittedly engineered, sickened me."

Cyntia shrugged, as if my evaluation of her morality meant nothing. "The purpose, your purpose, must always be your choice. And yet, it is our job to create the bowl that holds those experiences. You are not just a young man." She sighed then, resettling those ancient hands. "Come now. We are Spirit Marga, Ianto. In the end, we serve humanity even in all its new forms. You are a vowed monk. Yield."

I thought of kneeling before Vic in the woods, the knife between us. That surrender had been easy, a falling into a kind of grace. This felt different, and part of me roiled with an anger so intense that it threatened to push my body into action against the venerable old lady.

She seemed to read my face, and tipped forward at her waist. "Do you feel it?" she asked. "The carrier signal should be back on--can you isolate it?"

I looked at her then, anger vying with trying to make sense of her words. "No," I said.

"Try harder," she demanded. "You were able to identify a signal like it, just months ago, when all the Children of God were echoing each other, moving as a single organism."

I flashed back to the Children of God moving as one, their rooms identically organized, their faces verging on a blankness that had been terrifying to see. "I didn't hear a signal; it was intuition. I felt nothing then, no mechanism at work."

"Yet, you were right about its genesis. Somehow you knew it, when you saw it. It is not a mechanism as such. At least, not a near source--it is more subtle than that," Cyntia said. "Feel for it."

I had no wish to comply with her demands, except for a perverse curiosity. I closed my eyes, trying to feel the familiar ping of electronics within. But I found only silence. If my body was being acted upon, I could not sense it.

The sound of a door opening snapped me back into the room. I turned and stiffened. Warren was entering the room, but he was not the Binder who had left just minutes before. His face was cold, his motions more feral and intense.

I glanced at Cyntia, and she merely nodded. "This is the Warren we can make. Unmake him, pull out the healer again."

"I don't know how. If you can stop this..."

Warren slipped along the wall behind me, and I turned toward him. I still could not feel anything unusual except the harsh wash of emotion pounding in my temples as I watched him move, his eyes hunting me. And the more I felt myself stiffen inside, the more agitated his own motions became.

"Submit," a voice echoed in my ear. I knew the rich tones, the hint of an accent, and the flash of golden hair out of the corner of my eye. "Submit and you will hear it."

I went to my knees then, hands in my lap. And Warren crossed the space between us in three quick strides. "That shit will not work with me. You are a monster. Stand," he growled.

I kept my gaze on his feet, kept opening to him. I tried to let myself become passive, soft, the hollow flute that Tebre had instructed me to become when I healed with her. And there, in my chest, I could feel a low level of agitation within me, an unease, a kind of dread.

Warren finally snarled and reached down for me. He hauled me to my feet his hand around my throat. I looked up at him, reached inside him, feeling his heart, the network of veins in his head. I could win. I could turn him off. It would be a kindness, I thought. Blooded Binders were addicts, killers. I could give him a permanent peace.

"Soften," the voice came again.

Soften? I wanted to kill. I wanted to lash out. But slowly, I tipped my head to the side, my neck exposed, surrendering to him though it took every bit of self- control I had left. I could truly feel it then, like a noise barely within the range of hearing, more of a pressure in the ear and heart than an actual noise. I let myself go slack, let the noise echo through me instead of within me. I could feel the bits of Warren within me, and it was like I could tune them to the sound as well. Dimly, I felt Warren begin to tighten his grip.

But then he stopped.   And let me go. "Ianto?" he asked, his voice ragged.

I raised my face to him, feeling the blood pound at my neck where his fingers had pressed. "It's not you, Warren. Look at me. This is not you. And not me. They play us from without. Feel the sensation, soften to it. If you struggle, that feeds it. Feel the pressure."

Warren stared down at me, his eyes widened. "Something is pushing me," he said.

I nodded. "But you feel it now. And you know it's not you." I reached down and lifted his hand to the bruises at my neck. "This is you."

I could feel him cooling the skin, my hand over his. I felt a moment of radiance, as if both of us united and locked the world out. And the pressure eased. We did not stop it; we merely were aware and that awareness returned us to ourselves.

We turned our eyes to Cyntia. Mine, at least were filled with loathing for her. But she simply smiled and nodded.

Chapter 40

I would have liked history to remember me as a crafter of poetry, a writer of liturgy, perhaps even a fine mother. But that was never my lot. I was, instead, a chess player in the end. But nobody would ever know how I wept for the pawns in my isolation. How I weep still.

Drunken Days
High Priestess Cyntia Molair

We waited there in the living room of the lodge, Warren and I, warily watching Cyntia. She continued to smile to herself, her sharp eyes studying us with great interest. "I knew you would be able to shield yourself from our "push" as you called it. But to be able to extend that to Warren, to wake him up as well! That was remarkable."

I shook my head. "Warren sensed it on his own; I did nothing."

"No, Ianto. He attuned himself to you. You broke through to him. I saw it with my own eyes. Fascinating." She stood then. "I will call Leland and have him return you to your monastery."

Warren frowned. "That's it? All this, these months in the woods, the deaths. You just call a driver and take us home?"

Cyntia looked at him, her eyes soft and almost compassionate. I wasn't sure I liked that look any more than when she had been dissecting us both in a glance. "Leland will drive Ianto home, Warren. Not you. I will have another driver take you to the Temple to serve on the healing staff there. You will be able to help recognize outside influences on the staff that are Children of God--I believe they called it a canary in the mine. Now that Ianto has tuned you, so to speak, I believe you will sense other such intrusions in time." She smiled as she looked up at the towering Binder, affectionate almost.

It only made me more uncomfortable, watching her using her words and expressions like old fashioned playing cards.

"And Tebre?" I asked carefully. "What has happened to her?"

"She will join Warren at the Temple for the time being," Cyntia replied. "She is an amazing Child of God, an able healer, and as singularly difficult to push as yourself. We have offered her a job of sorts, and she was eager to take it as long as Warren would be with her." Cyntia smiled at Warren. "I think," she said, "Tebre is in love."

Warren merely frowned, his red eyes downcast.

"And what am I to do at the monastery?" I asked, letting frost come out again. "Pray about all this?"

Cyntia grinned at him. "You will be trained, Ianto. Trained to be able to protect our Children of God from outside influences, trained to shut things off as needed, trained to begin to better understand the world we move through, and your role in its forward movement through time. We begin immediately to refine your purpose with us."

I know she did not miss the set in my face, the hardness of my gaze. "High Priestess," I said, biting out each word, "I am prepared to revoke my vows now, before you with Warren as witness." I glared at her then, defiant.

"Be very careful, Ianto," she said. She walked toward me slowly and I had to fight the urge to drop my gaze from her. "You are so young and so naïve. Word of your abilities has leaked out from the time you made your way out of the research facility. Do you know that Spirit Marga has repulsed not less than six offers of purchase for you, some for more money than a year's earnings of the entire Marga? That Hobert and Leland have successfully disarmed three separate attempts to take you from the monastery by force?"

I blinked quickly, absorbing her words.

"You leave the Spirit Marga and you will not be left free in this world. I can offer you some semblance of freedom, but the forces in play right now, if they take you, will not be so kind. We offer you a safe haven, training to rise to your potential, companionship, a faith and community. They would offer you exactly what they would offer a lab rat. They would find ways to bend you that you cannot even imagine; for some, harvesting your nanotech and beginning biological research on your brain and nervous system is a high priority. You think us manipulative and arrogant. Maybe even see us as monsters; yes, it's written all over your face. But I am telling you, we are the only ones who can also protect you." Her shoulders dropped a little, her gaze less intense. "Go. Of course, go if you wish. But I would not see you end your life strapped to a table and treated as a science experiment."

She did not wait for me to comment. I felt Warren shift beside me, dazed at her words. She turned away, touching a small pin at her neck and speaking to someone we could not hear. Moments later, Leland entered the room through the porch door. He had changed to his green hermit robes, though a sidearm was strapped to his trim waist. A young woman in administrator blue robes entered with him.

"Warren, this is priestess T'mel. She will convey you to the Temple to begin your new assignment." Leland nodded at T'mel, who in turned bowed to Warren. When her head lifted, she looked at me keenly, her brown eyes full of unasked questions. Just as quickly, she looked away and gestured for Warren to come with her.

Warren glanced down at me. I could sense he wanted to stay by my side, even, I realized with a start, to protect me. I reached out and touched his arm. "I love Tebre as you do," I said quietly. "Don't leave her alone."

The Binder sagged a little then, but his red eyes were still fierce. "If you need me..."

"I'll find you," I answered. "Somehow."

"What will you do now, Ianto?" he asked. "Do you believe what they are telling you?"

I shook my head, the words like lab rat and bending still rattling around in my skull. "It is not out of the realm of possibility. Go with God, Warren."

He nodded and turned to follow T'mel, but not without a quick backward glance through the doorframe. He finally ducked through, and for a moment, I felt naked and alone.

Leland tipped his head to one side, his dark eyes considering me. "You're looking a lot better," he said. "And you seem to have made friends with the boogie man himself."

"Turns out, it wasn't really Warren I should have feared," I said quietly. "Is it true?"

"What?" Leland asked. He looked less intimidating in his habit, his short spiky hair at odds with his relaxed frame.

"That Hobert and you have had to repel outside...." I stopped fumbling for my words.

"Attempts to acquire you?" he asked with a lopsided grin. "A few times. Luckily, we have very good intelligence. That, and any mechanical implements coming close to your hermitage registered on our board. Your self-imposed no-technology zone proved to be a great backdrop for picking up any unusual activity."

"I never felt them," I said soberly.

"Technology moves ahead like that. I wouldn't let it bother you. Cyntia believes you'll simply become more sensitive with time. I think we've been lucky that nobody has tried to just kill you and take the little beasties inside your head. Doesn't mean they won't try that soon. I'm not sure all of them think they necessarily need *you* alive to do the things Cyntia thinks they want you for."

I swallowed with a nod. "We should go," I said.

"Yes we should. This way," Leland gestured.

I looked over at Cyntia who had moved to the back of the living room and was studying the pines. "Should she be here alone?" I asked quietly.

Leland chuckled. "You really can't tell, can you? She's not here at all," he said. "At least not in the flesh so to speak. She's the head of Spirit Marga; traveling around to maintain a world-wide organization is not exactly an efficient option for her."

Before my eyes, her image shimmered and then faded.

"Holotechnology?" I asked, stunned. "But the transmitter...I couldn't sense it."

He looked at me carefully then shrugged his shoulders. "Sort of. Our techs can feed her image through your nanotech, and the ones other select people and I have had implanted. It feels like she is here, but she's never left her office."

"I should still be able to sense that," I said to him. I could feel my heart pounding. "Why can't I?"

"Not enough training yet? Not knowing how to feel for it? I don't know," Leland said with a shrug. "Though I suspect you'll learn."

"Leland?" I asked. "Do you think Spirit Marga has been transmitting other people to me?" I called up his image in my mind, the blond hair, his delicate tipped ears and flashing blue eyes. Part of me tightened inside, unwilling to believe that the spirit, the gentle and tormented presence I had felt for the past months, was only another projection from the Marga. Or maybe worse, that it rose from some other source.

Leland frowned deeply. "Nothing I know of. Have you experienced this kind of technology before?"

"Something like this," I said, my eyes straying to where Cyntia had stood moments before. "Not the same, though. I can reach back through to...somewhere, and sometimes it reaches through to me. And it's highly localized.

To the best of my knowledge, I'm the only one who experiences it."

"I wouldn't encourage you *reaching* anywhere," Leland said, his eyes suddenly hooded and on guard. "There may be more than one way of acquiring you. Like I said, technology changes fast. I'll need to report this."

I closed my eyes for a moment, trying to feel into the room. But I could only sense the warmth of the sunlight through the high windows, the smell of old cedar and wood smoke. If there was another kind of push or carrier signal, I could not sense it.

"So do I take you home?" he finally asked me.

I nodded, too lost in thought to interact anymore.

Chapter 41

*We are called to be obedient. The only
problem arises when we ask obedient to
whom? That is the question our conditioning
beats back. Our eyes and hearts are carefully
directed, our ears stuffed so we will not stray
off the course. I remember reading that
stallions once had their noses coated with
eucalyptus oil so mares in heat wouldn't
bother them, so they would perform with
attention. I know the technique still applies
to us. If I could simply accept that my life is
not my own, it would be better. But I am
beginning to see the structure of our
obedience. And to hear the whispers of that
one, terrible question...obedient to whom?*

*Personal Writings
Priest-Commander Leland*

I opened the door of the transport, and
stopped cold. My hood lay on the passenger seat,
blue fabric and the fine mesh catching the
afternoon light. Leland looked at me over the top
of the vehicle and read my expression with ease.

"Hobert is putting a number of other monks in full habits. Decoys. He asks that you wear it again. We won't be going back to your old hermitage, but one like it nearby. They're all the same, really, on the inside."

I picked up the fabric, running my thumb over the mesh. "Yes. Except for the gardens. But then, mine has probably gone to weeds."

"Jean watched over it for you," Leland said. He opened the transport door and slipped inside. I followed him, laying the hood on my lap. The mention of her name brought with it a strange wave of emotion. Anger, certainly, at her part in the deception of the past months. Memories of our easy years together, then the unplanned lovemaking in the woods rose up sharp. It all mixed together in me, complex and gray. I did not desire her. But I did miss her, in spite of my anger.

Leland glanced at me as he started the transport. "She's her mother's daughter, Ianto, born and bred to serve the Marga before all else. You begin to understand, yes?"

"Yes." But of course it was a lie. I felt like I understood nothing.

Leland turned down the two-track, adjusting a number of controls. "Heat OK? These damn woods chill me to the bone. I feel like I'm never going to be warm again."

"I'm fine," I answered, looking out the window as the trees and ferns and mossy rocks slipped past in both endless monotony and endless variety. The controls he had touched had nothing to do with heat. I could feel an electronic web of some sort ease around the contours of the transport.

"It's going to be a very long ride if you answer everything in less than a sentence," he said, giving me a short smile. Then he sighed, shaking his head. "I'm sorry. Hell, it's OK if you want to catch some sleep. You've been through a lot. But I've got your back here. Hours of road ahead."

"I'm fine," I said again.

Leland leaned a bit on the armrest between us, steering over the gravel road with a practiced ease. Out of the corner of my eye, I saw him frown a little. "I doubt you're as OK as you say," he said quietly. "I wouldn't be, not by a long shot."

I didn't answer him.

We drove along like that for a long time, his eyes watching the road, mine the passing and thinning woods. It wasn't long before we turned on to pavement. In the distance, I could see the shoulders of mountains, only the tops frosted with white. Leland smiled in appreciation of the view. "Never get tired of them," he said.

"No. They're lovely." But my voice and my enthusiasm were both flat. I shifted a bit, so I could see him more clearly in profile. He shifted at first, feeling my eyes on him. "Something wrong?" he asked.

"Do you understand what all of this is for?" I asked quietly.

"All of this is a bit, um, vague, Ianto."

"The tests. The threats. Now the stronger security, when you were perfectly happy letting me run in the woods for months. I felt at least one shield of some sort come down over this transport. That's not normal, is it?"

He chuckled. "And you have to ask why, after that last observation of yours? Nobody can do what you do, Ianto. And we don't know what else you can do; some techs think you're just starting to come into your potential. As I understand it, the Margas are pretty excited about you, and well, pretty terrified, too." He shrugged as if he didn't share that fear.

"As I told Cyntia, I'm one person. Not a threat. Not a prodigy."

"No, my friend, you're wrong there." He shifted a bit, switching hands at the steering wheel.

I dropped my gaze to my lap, to the hood that still tangled in my fingers. "Warren spoke of great ships, that somehow the Children of God would be...encouraged to leave here and make the crossings. But there's fear at the heart of it, like the ships will...atone for something. How am I part of all that? Why would my particular...abnormalities...be useful?" I hated my halting voice, the thick, stressed lines of thought that almost gagged me.

Leland shrugged. "That is something I can't really address with you. Someday, soon, when I have permission." He looked at me quickly then back at the road. "I can tell you that they think you can stabilize something to do with the ships, the primary guidance and command systems. But I don't know details."

I shook my head. "I don't work with computers."

"No. I know. You'll just have to be patient."

"Would you be?" I asked quickly and with more anger than Leland deserved.

He gazed at me, then back to the road. "Probably not," he said, after a long pause.

A light flashed on his flat systems board in front of him. I watched him touch a small tab at his collar and could tell by his sudden frown and stiffening spine that someone was conveying information that he did not like. He blinked quickly and then listened for quite a while before he signed off without a word.

"Trouble?" I asked.

His head turned, gauging the road. "Not for us. At least not yet." I watched his fingers flex hard against the steering wheel. He drew his breath in deeply through his nose then. We pulled off the main highway, dipping back into the forest on a two-lane road. I stayed silent, observing, but feeling a familiar knot in my stomach, a knot with roots clear back to my childhood.

"The transport carrying Warren and my assistant was hit by a heavy hauler, farther up the road," Leland said, his voice deliberately flat. "It shoved their vehicle over the embankment. Long drop there. My people say it was not an accident. They were both killed."

I closed my eyes, willing imaginary pictures of their fall from my mind.

Warren.

I bit down on my emotions, like biting on a stick to ease pain.

"I'm sorry," he said. I could hear his teeth grinding as he struggled with his own rage and impotence. "God, there're so few Binders with his skill sets. To lose one like this..."

"He would have been my friend, I think. One day." My voice sounded hollow.

He nodded. "I'm sorry," he said again, his voice softer.

"Why? Why hit *his* transport?" I spit out. I felt suddenly like a caged animal, the dash and seat and belts ensnaring me. I kicked the floorboards savagely.

Leland stared straight ahead, his cheekbones standing out harshly under the tightened skin of his face. "It may have been aimed at you," he said. "We don't know for sure. Same make and model of transport, same color, same Spirit Marga signatures; they might have thought...." He frowned then, and pulled over to the side of the road. He called for a map of the area, and enlarged it to fill the entire clear dash area.

I saw what he saw immediately. This road, the only one feeding onto the highway for over forty miles, angled back up into the mountains and dissolved quickly into a series of switchbacks with the satellite image of runnels of driveways leading to isolated mountain summer homes. It was both rough and beautifully positioned for anyone hoping to stop a vehicle.

"I don't like this," he said. He raised his eyes, scanning the empty road. "I don't like this one damn bit."

"So backtrack," I said, tracing my finger down the road, to the highway, and back to another road system with healthy intersections and fewer twists. "We can take this route here. Follow it over to this other north-south roadway. More options. This one is like a canyon further on."

"I'm probably just being paranoid," Leland said. His eyes glared down the road as if he could make it something other than what it was.

I cocked my head, listening to the ping and hiss of the carrier signal around me. "I hear the Spirit Marga tracker. I can break it. That will make us less easy to find."

Leland struggled with his thoughts for a moment.

"Leland?"

"If you break it, we run without the Marga being able to track us. They may think we've been hit," he said cautiously.

"A Spirit Marga signal didn't save Warren," I said, the edge of bitterness in my voice.

Warren.

Dead.

He hesitated only a moment more. "Do it," he said tightly.

So I did.

He backed us around, and sped up to the highway. Night was beginning to fall, streaking the sky with reds and golds, but also shadowing the roadway and the forest just beyond our headlights.

"Is the transport charge going to last?" I asked.

"I think so," he said, his eyes on the road again. He turned onto the northbound highway and set his controls for the new route. "More damn woods," he sighed.

Warren's face kept coming up in my mind. I finally leaned my head back and shut my eyes. I feathered my internal senses out and around us, but the speed and the electronic noise of the transport kept me blind. So I tried to let the sway, the motion, carry me into a place of calm.

It didn't work.

Chapter 42

It is no accident that the mother of Yeshua played such a central role in the old Christian faith. I look around, and all I see are the mothers of inventions, of personalities, of dreams. In this fabulous birthing of creativity, even the occasional stillborn lowered into the dirt seems to feed the towering trees themselves. A mother put the Game in motion. A mother birthed the antidote to the Game. A mother killed from within it and without. Everywhere, the face of Mary, regardless of gender. We women are the very ground of religion, and the binding back we do in our own hearts and minds is staggering. It is terrible and it is holy.

Drunken Days
High Priestess Cyntia Molair

Leland pulled into a travelers' station after three hours on the road. I could tell from the dark circles under his eyes and the way he gripped the wheel that more than our transport needed a recharge. He flipped the holster of his gun open, gestured for me to stay put, then stepped out and slowly pulled the plug-line from the front of our vehicle. After tapping in his pass code, he settled the link into the charge pod. I could hear the faint hum as our vehicle started to power up.

He straightened then, his keen eyes scanning the parking lot, then gestured for me to follow. I stepped out on the pavement, blinking a little in the harsh white glare of what served as both a diner and service station. A mother, with her child in tow, cast us a quick glance and then a somewhat longer stare before she hurried her child inside the building. I suppose our strange clothing, and Leland's weapon strapped so incongruously to his waist, would have made anyone curious. Or damn nervous.

"Restroom break. Get food to take with you if you are hungry," Leland said. "We're on pod six; just direct the auto-checkout to charge the food to that account."

I looked at him blankly.

He started to say something, most likely impatiently, but seemed to catch himself and shook his head instead. "I'm sorry. I forget how little you've been out in the real world," he said. "Come on."

He took my elbow for a moment, but I shook him off with a gentle shrug.

The traveler's station was a riot of electronic menus and goods rosters scrolling across the walls of a relative empty space. I nodded politely to the woman and her child sitting in a hard plastic booth, but she did not return the gesture. Leland touched a menu screen, searched quickly and ordered coffee, a bag of mixed fruit and nuts, and entered his code. Moments later, his request was dispensed from a panel that opened up beneath the menu. If there was a human being on the other side, I couldn't sense him or her.

"Ianto? What do you want? Coffee?"

I shook my head, captivated by the menus scrolling past...Indian food, Tai, Chinese, pizza all racing by. I didn't know there were so many kinds of food in the world. And on another screen, row after row of topics ranging from music to condoms to I. L. batteries for the transports whipped by. Much of it, I couldn't even identify. I could feel the woman watching us, though. It all gave me a vague headache.

"Ianto!"

"Juice," I answered without looking at Leland.

"You have to eat something."

"Not hungry," I said.

"You get any gaunter and Hobert is going to strap you down and force feed you."

"You know that doesn't work," I said absently, eyes still moving over the riot of symbols and color.

"All right. Go use the bathroom, and let's get out of here. The transport should be charged and ready for the next ten to twelve hours of driving ahead of us. Ianto! Now would be good." Leland barked.

I shook my head, clearing it, and did as he asked.

When I re-entered the main vending room, I found myself again entranced with the displays, held as much by the play of light over my eyes as by the words spelling out mysteries I had never experienced in my circumscribed life. I stood in the middle of it all, the screens of information flicking by, the tickle and low whine in my ears from the electronics of the place. I felt if I could relax just a little, the information could stream right into me, sweet and warm and fulfilling. The room seemed to tilt a bit, and then Leland's face was superimposed over the menu. "What's wrong?"

"So rich," I heard myself slur.

"My God, you sound drunk." Leland took my arm and tried to gently propel me to the door.

I couldn't move. The lights, the flow of data, were all so lovely. He was right. I was intoxicated, enraptured.

"Ianto, we don't have time for this. We need to get back in the transport." I think he shook me then, enough that my teeth clicked a bit. But that observation itself seemed very far away.

However, when he slapped me, I must say that registered for at least a moment. I blinked quickly, looking into his eyes, feeling like I had a small window out into reality, a window was rapidly closing again. "That was rude, Leland," I heard myself whisper. And then I was drowning again, my focus swimming in ecstatic light and sensation until I could not tell floor from ceiling from wall.

The next thing I knew, I was on the pavement in the empty parking lot, Leland kneeling beside me, breathing hard. I looked around, confused, and then rolled over to my side and promptly threw up.

Leland turned his head aside, grimacing. "What the hell was that? It was like you were mainlining all that data; like it was some kind of drug." Leland rolled me away from the mess, and held me there, one hand smoothing back the sweaty strands of hair from my face. I took slow, even breaths, allowing the world to solidify and make sense again around me.

"I'm OK," I said at last. But I felt anything but OK. My stomach and I had a very uneasy truth, and I could feel a terrible pressure behind my eyes.

"Yeah, right. Remind me not to ever take you anywhere near a world market center. We need to get you in the transport. Now." Leland tugged a bit at me, and I sat up and got slowly to my feet. Two sets of headlights flared into the parking lot. We both spared them only a glance, and turned toward our vehicle. I had only taken a few steps when a familiar tickle inside me made me stumble and then draw up. "Warren?" I pivoted slowly toward the vehicles by charge pods at the other end of the travel center.

Leland jerked at my arm. "Did you just say Warren?" He followed my gaze, his hand tightening. "Now, Ianto. I need you in that transport now."

I watched a man get out of one vehicle. He was slight, with a cap jammed over his head and an open-front coat riding his narrow hips. I could feel the tickle of a ping inside of me, and my eyes widened in confusion.

The man reached inside his coat, pulled out a weapon and fired even as Leland threw us both to the ground. Our transport window shattered above and behind us.

I realized, in that moment, it was not Warren I sensed, but someone who had been very close to him recently. The tension and the lingering euphoria all came crashing together. I snapped out my hand, reacting out of rage and without thought. Everything I could reach into exploded. The lights around the parking lot flared then shattered, and the two transports lurched as if hit by an invisible hand. The automated doors of the travel station trembled with a blast from inside the building. But mostly, I could see the man who had shot at us hit the ground face first. He didn't even try to break his fall. Beyond him, I caught the faint signature of others in the second transport, fading now, already broken. As quickly as it had come, the destruction stopped, everything settling down into small sparks.

In the sudden quiet and darkness, I could hear Leland's ragged breath. "Holy ones of many lands, I had no idea," he murmured. "No idea."

I got to my feet, leaving him still kneeling and shocked by our transport. I stumbled toward the downed gunman. Dark liquid had pooled around his head. I opened my palm and could feel the fading echo. I was right. He had been around Warren, and recently. I felt the incredibly small fragments of the Binder vibrating with an intensity that was new, vibrating like a warning. Perhaps that is why I heard them so clearly. They reach out to me, like pieces of orphaned consciousness lost and alone. And something in me reached out and welcomed them home.

I could feel Leland watching me with eyes that were no longer so naïve about why people might want me for their own purposes, or failing that, just want me dead. And as always, the terrible loneliness closed in and nearly took my breath away.

I walked slowly back to the transport, watching Leland climb cautiously to his feet. I stopped a few feet away. "You saved my life," I said quietly.

Leland simply shook his head. I stood very close to him now, watching him carefully. He still looked dazed.

"If they had come when I was still in there," I gestured with my head toward the now-dark travelers' stop, "I wouldn't have been able to stop them from shooting me, us. So learn this now. I am not omnipotent, Leland. I have a skill, one that I am still learning to use and that's all." I could hear the intensity of my own voice, the need to be understood. "So how many more tests will it take to prove that? How many more people should I kill for you, how much more property would you like destroyed? Was it interesting for you to see that strobed data is a weapon against me? Have you already added that to my file somewhere?"

Leland started to open his mouth then, but I cut him off with a look. "One transport, one driver with one little gun? Hours of open road, a transport blaring our Spirit Marga signal? Convenient back tracking, a friend maybe dead, maybe not, because I don't always catch when I am being lied to. You could call in enough support to take over the state, am I right? I'm not stupid, Leland. And all this is transparent." I cocked my head, a Binder affectation that I had recently picked up. "Did you want more data? Or did you just want me dead? Or did *they* want you dead for some reason so they set you up to die? Talk to me, Leland. Explain it to me."

Leland's face was finding its composure. That alone told me he had known how at least some of this would go down. He flared his nostrils, drawing in a deep breath. "Rural. Semi-urban. Deep city. We didn't know how you would react in each scenario. Yes, the data stream working on you like a drug was something we had not anticipated, and the ramifications of that weakness will need to be explored because it can be used against you or compromise your ability to act in certain environments. Over-reactions, too, are problematic with you. There are times when you don't seem to exercise any degree of focused ability, and the strength of your reactions tends to correspond directly to your mental and emotional states, which is another level of control over you that can be utilized. Deep bonding is also problematic for you, and it is becoming more and clearer that even relatively mild bonds of any kind skew your behavior in a crisis."

"Utilized." I caught that one word out of the flurry of words. My eyes drifted over to the body by the parked transports. I couldn't see the other two dead in the second transport, but I had been within them. "Were these people correctly *utilized*, Leland? Were you? Seems almost everything you have learned about me you could have guessed. I'm pretty human, after all. I take care of my friends and over-react when I am about to be shot in cold blood. That's not exactly hard to figure out, is it? Unless you are the ones having trouble with basic human behavior." I was cold inside, but not even cold rage. Rather, it felt like a necessary flatness was growing in my mind, creating shields I could hide behind.

"Guessing is not the same as observation," Leland said. He snapped his holster shut without looking down. "Come here. I want to show you something."

I looked again at the dead man in the drive, and wondered when the next transport would pull into the parking lot.

"There won't be any more transports here tonight," he said, reading my glance. "The road is blocked at both ends. There will be teams coming in by air shortly. They'll clean this up."

"And Warren?"

Leland paused a moment, then shook his head. He wouldn't even meet my eye.

"Why?"

"I'm not party to such things."

"Even if you are implicated in them?"

"Let me show you something" Leland said, and then moved around to the passenger side and unsnapped a small piece of equipment from the dash. He walked a little into the darkness beside the travel shop and touched a button. A three-dimensional image flared into shape. Despite my anger, I was curious and moved to where I could better see it.

It was an image of a vast ship, if the size of the windows and cargo bay door told anything about its scale. Low and flat, it hung in a sea of stars. I glanced up at the sky almost expecting to see through the cloud cover. "What is it?" I asked quietly.

"Just what it looks like. A generation ship, assembled by the Spirit and Science Margas and with the help of the Emperium. It's called the Operator, and she's ready to fly. Has been for years. All she needs is a crew; the right crew, Ianto, and a guiding mind that will see her safely from Earth to her new berth three human generations away. You are one of a handful of Children of God being tested to be on that team that will hold all the lives that will fill that ship. That's all I really know."

I looked at the ship, stunned by its size, and by its sudden reality.

"Will you get in trouble for showing me this?" I asked. My eyes swept the enormous ship again, drinking in her long lines, the heavy gray of her skin.

"I was told to," Leland answered, touching the little tab in his ear.

Chapter 43

I do appreciate the idea of free will and choice so championed by the Spirit Marga. Such ideas make one feel powerful, in control. And as long as not too many take them seriously, they can be very useful tools even for our Game creations who supposedly have no souls or wills of their own.

AI Design and Implementation
Petrek, Emperium Tech Grade 1

Leland snapped the image off, and I blinked a few times, my mind afire with questions. But he raised his hand, shaking his head. "I don't know any more than what I've told you, so don't ask."

I nodded mutely, then a tickle of memory turned my eyes toward the travel center. "Leland," I asked with a frown. "Did they get out?"

"Did who get out?" he asked.

"The mother and her child. Did they get out?" I started walking briskly toward the dark building, without waiting for his reply.

"Ianto!"

I broke into a run. No. I couldn't have killed them, too. A little girl. Her mother. Memories of another little girl in the rain, broken on my lap, rose fresh and painful in me. As I reached my hand to shove aside the door, it opened from within. I stumbled back, surprised. The woman, too, drew up with a sharp breath. She was very pale, her eyes large and dark, her hair bobbed short and curly. The little girl hovered behind her, making little whimpering sounds. "Sorry," she said. "There was some kind of mechanical failure and..."

Her eyes fell on the dead man in the parking lot and she froze. "Is he...?"

"Yes. An accident," I said. "But everything's OK now."

She nodded, her eyes still wide and she swallowed convulsively.

"The road is blocked at both ends. You might want to stay inside the building until help arrives." I smiled down at her, to reassure her that all was well, and gestured for her to return to the building.

Abruptly, she reached out and grasped the fabric of my sleeve. Her voice was soft, conspiratorial. "You need to come back inside with me, Ianto. You've caused quite a mess and nearly blown us all to the next life. I would say such pyrotechnics truly make you your mother's son, but you don't know all that much about her, do you? Not really."

I felt the smile slip from my face.

"I have two men holding controls for bombs to this place. If their hearts stop, the bombs go off. If you try to tamper with the bombs using your skill as you call it, they will go off."

"You'll die," I murmured stupidly.

"Most likely," she said quietly. "As will my daughter. And that man you're with...Leland, is it? I don't think you want more innocent lives on your hands."

I shook my head. "Who are you?" I felt my weight come up on my toes, a reaction I had learned in the deep forest when stress hit. What had the ancient psychologists called it? Fight or flight?

She smiled sweetly up at me, her eyes so wide and practical then she might as well have struck me. "I'm on a mission from your mother. And if that isn't incentive enough for a short conversation, then think of the trauma you would cause this child. Oh," she said, tugging at my sleeve as if sharing a joke, "in case Spirit Marga has succeeded in making you a sociopath and you are only adding up non-Marga casualties like a computer, if *I* stop breathing, the bomb also goes off."

I stared at her, my muscles frozen. My mother? I could see a flash of her in my mind, dead from an overdose. And then I could feel Leland begin moving toward us, his heart rate accelerating.

"Are they OK? Ianto?" Leland called.

I blinked quickly. "What do you want?" I asked, shifting so I could shield her from Leland's gaze. "Fast. Now."

"Come back through these doors with me. Just step through." She turned and shooed her child ahead of her.

I looked at Leland and he read my face flawlessly. "Ianto! No, don't! Stop there! No!"

I shook my head and stepped through the doorway. The woman hit the lockdown pad. It had been hastily installed, and I knew it had been right there in front of our eyes minutes before and we just hadn't registered it. A secondary metal door slid obediently into place. Moments later, I could hear the dull clangs as Leland beat on the door from the outside.

She guided her daughter to what was left of the plastic table, wiping a bit at it with her hand. The monitors that used to make up the walls had all gone dark, and only a small light glowed from a hand-held torch that she had placed on the tabletop.

I still stood by the doorway, watching her.

"This will only take a moment, Ianto. Then, if you wish, you can join your friend before he breaks his hand on that door." She opened a small hard-sided briefcase, pulled out a strange glove. It was bright white, with black nubs set almost like grips along the palm and fingers. "What are you doing?" I asked without moving.

"Don't you mean, how do I know your mother?" She smiled again at me as she settled the glove on her hand and tightened down the wrist strap.

"I don't care about what you can tell me," I said and was surprised that I meant it. "Stories are not reality."

"And even reality itself can be bent, is that what you are saying? Like glass walls?" She gestured to me. "Come on, then."

I walked over to her slowly, to that small circle of light rimming the table.

"I used to work with your mother. Lucy there," she nodded to the little girl who continued to sniffle and watch us with wide eyes, "is your age."

"What?" I looked at her again, but all I could see was a child of about four.

"Your mother and I were in genetic development together, and both decided we had no need of husbands. We each created a child that would suit our needs. Me? I didn't want a child who would grow up and leave me. I love this age, even," she said with a small wince, "when Lucy gets so clingy."

"I don't..."

"Believe me? That's quite all right. Your mother was my best friend, and I was very hurt when she decided to take you and play neo-hippie in the woods." She shook her head. "I love the underground cities; can't imagine going native wrapped around with all that space. In any case, she charged me with giving you a choice when you came of age if she could not. That is what I am doing here. Both my job, and offering you the choice your mother wanted you to have. Two birds, one stone, as they used to say."

"Your job? A choice? You're not making sense." I stayed just out of reach of her, feeling into her, reading her in all the ways open to me. She was so calm, so steady, even knowing I could kill her and her child. That calm baffled me.

"Some things take time to make sense, Ianto." She held out her hand that was clothed in the strange glove. "Just take my hand. One quick squeeze."

"No," I backed a step away. "Answer my questions."

"And how do you know that I won't simply lie to you?" She raised her perfectly sculpted eyebrows and smiled again. "Can you accept the truth as truth? I'm not sure you can, you see, so that is why I hesitate to tell you anything."

"Try me," I said, keeping my voice as calm as I could.

She shook her head, considering me. "Very well," she said at last. "As you may be figuring out by now, your mother made you to be extraordinary. Nerves that were designed to interface with technology that was still in its infancy. She didn't want you to have the first generation of nanotech that the Margas were pushing. She wanted you to wait, to be something quite different from a passive acceptor of information. She wanted you to be able to send information out as well. And then, as you grew, she became afraid of what that skill might mean. How others would want to use it, control it."

"Then why did she kill herself? Why didn't she help me?" I blurted out the words, like they had always waited there, in the back of my throat.

"Because she was a bipolar genius who could hardly stand her own mind. I'm sure it had nothing to do with *you*, Ianto. In fact, I am pretty sure she deeply loved you, as much as that woman could love anyone. Her mind, her mind, Ianto! It was a miracle and a prison for her. And so, she asked me if I would give you a choice when you came of age, a simple choice, in case your life had become as, well, strained as her own did on occasion."

She raised the glove. "This will sample your DNA, your body's chemical reactions and hopefully capture a few stray bits of your nanotech load. I know you can send them out and re-home them, by the way. We've been able to make certain hypotheses based on intercepted data over the past few years. Although this," she said with a wave of her free hand, "was beyond anything we had imagined you could do. I think it means you are tapping the nanotech that have been multiplying in the environment, which means you are growing as fast within as they are without. How long until you will sense things miles from you? How long until this whole world becomes an extension of your own senses? And your reaction to the dataflow inside this station? Fascinating! I can't begin to imagine what you may be capable of if you can interface with other kinds of input. If your gift can be replicated..."

"You want to replicate what I am?" I asked, cutting her off. I took another step back.

"Not entirely, no. We want to understand you, Ianto, and make improvements, tamp down some of the more creative or reactionary parts of yourself if we do decide to continue your genetic line. Spirit Marga is beside itself over you because they know they might have a pilot for their big hulk of a ship a generation ahead of when they thought something like you would ready, and at the same time, they also know they are sitting on a human time bomb. They don't know how to control you well, to keep you from hurting yourself or others. Your reactions are not cleanly predictable, which drives them crazy. You have great potential" she said with great earnestness. "Unfortunately, all in a package that is, well, far too human really. If we are successful at unpacking how this all works it eventually gets you off the hook and out from under the microscope. Understand? Maybe we can make you obsolete, which in this case is a good thing indeed."

I kept easing my way back from her, keeping her where I could see her, and began to reach out with my mind for the doorway relays.

She didn't pursue me. In fact, her face and blood pressure had hardy changed at all. "Ianto, there has been some suggestion that you have been having visions over the years, yes? I think I know who or maybe what you are seeing. It's just a guess, really. But an educated one. I happen to know that forces are in play that will take his life, not today, but in the near future. If you will just take my hand, maybe they will find something that will make him of continued value as well."

I frankly stared at her. "But how..."

"Because I am one of the people who has worked with your blond elf from the time he was injured as a child."

"Who? Who is he?" I stopped my slow retreat.

"It's not time for you to learn that yet. And besides, it's more a question of *where* is he, even more so than whom. You can't even begin to ask the right questions, so you're not ready." She sighed. "This test will help us to clarify the puzzle that is you, and why you are growing toward him, toward your vision of him in any case. Please, Ianto. There is little time left. Please. Take my hand."

I looked again at the glove that hovered ghost-like in the near dark. "You said my mother was offering me a choice. Is this--this other man in my mind--is this part of that choice?"

She looked at me thoughtfully. "Actually, I suppose it is in a way."

We both heard a low roar begin outside, air transports from Spirit Marga, their mechanical power shaking the walls of the travel center. The woman looked speculatively around the room then refocused on me.

"We're out of time, Ianto," she said. "Please. Take my hand. Take my hand and you can save all those lives out there. Because you know they will try to get you out. You know they will set off the bombs. Is this how you want us all to die? It would be such a waste, in truth."

I looked into her eyes, troubled that her heart rate still had not changed. She reached out her hand, and my gaze fell to it again. "I'm not sure I care anymore," I answered her quietly. "Every turn I make has been pre-destined for me. I have no ground to stand on. Never. Dying does not frighten me." I looked again at the door. "But killing does."

"I know," she said softly.

I walked to her, and reached out for the white-gloved hand.

Chapter 44

You cannot imagine the delight when I found that the Spirit Marga's Ianto Tobali was indeed the child of one of our missing Techs, one who had worked very closely with me as I developed the entity called Nuress. I was quite aware that she had used her own profoundly advanced genetic work on her own son, and as I watched his growth from afar, I recognized the value of what she had created. Or rather, what we had created. I like to tinker— sometimes the sketches develop into something quite unexpected. And the touches I left within the genetic blueprint of her son would only flourish in the right environments, awaken at the right times. Since she first disappeared, I have kept an almost Spirit Marga sense that divine justice would bring the child back to me, wholly and finally.

Game Notes
Senior Developer Petrek

I took her hand, feeling hundreds of little barbs bury into the skin of my palm and wrist. I winced as she tightened her grip for just a moment, then she pulled back, pressing a tab on the glove. Moments later, it gave a little beep. "All done and transmitted," she said, carefully peeling the glove off.

"To where?" I asked.

She smiled, shaking her head. "The Emperium labs I would presume. Do you need a pad for your hand?" she asked.

I turned it over for her to see. The wounds closed neatly, leaving only smears of blood on my palm and wrist. The Binder in me was getting stronger and I didn't know how to feel about it.

She reached out for my hand again, brushing at the blood. "My, this is interesting, isn't it? Binder? This proves some of the theories. The techies will be so ecstatic with your data."

"So everyone says," I murmured, taking my hand back out of hers. "Now disarm the bomb."

"I can't," she said sadly. "Lucy, come here please."

The little girl scooted to her mother's side. She eyed me through her lashes, her eyes serious in a way that made her seem so much older. "Here's your treat, dear." The woman handed her a small candy disk, then popped one in her own mouth.

She handed one to me. "Don't eat it unless you want out."

"Out?" I asked.

She gestured around her. "Your mother wanted you to have a choice, if your life was not your own. A choice, but not to die alone. I said I would be there with you, right to the end of my own life. And so here we are." She crouched down and opened her arms. Her little girl fell into them, a habitual thumb edging toward her mouth as her eyes fell shut.

It took a couple of breaths to sink in. I stared at the candy. "Poison?"

"Yes. Bombs are a terribly messy way to go, don't you think? You have maybe a couple of minutes before..." she swayed and caught herself. "Probably not that."

There was one moment when I was tempted. One moment, but the thought of the people outside drove me to the door. "Code!"

"Be ...sure....Ianto."

"I've already told you. I'm not ready to die. Not like this. The code!

"007009." She lay down on the floor, cradling the rag doll form of her child. "007," she giggled weakly. "I hope..." her voice faded.

I tapped the numbers in, and burst through the door. "Bomb!" I yelled, grabbing at Leland's shoulder as I tore away from the building. I caught only a flash of the surprise on his face. "Everyone COVER!"

Leland and I sprinted across the gravel, my hand still clutching his shoulder. The two air transports stood hulking and gray by the edge of the highway. The men were scrambling to shelter behind them. We almost made it. Almost.

I can't remember the sound, just the sensation of being lifted and then flattened to the ground. The flames licked out over us, a red curtain, broiling, then lashed back the way they had come. We lay winded, our bodies scored by small rocks and debris. Leland gasped, rolling to his back, still coughing and wiping at the gravel burns on his face. I followed his lead, needing the sensation of space around me. It had been so close.

"Ianto..." he croaked out.

"Emperium agent. She's dead. Might be others in the woods," I answered, already knowing the questions behind the simple statement of my name. "And yes. I'm fine." Still coughing, I looked up into the blackness of the night sky, my knees bent, easing my back, feet to the ground. I barely registered the sudden press of men around us, checking our limbs, waving their fingers in front of our eyes, their movements crackling with adrenaline.

I hope, she had said. *I hope.* It echoed in my mind.

Chapter 45

The vocation of monk died out in the ancient times. Maybe the yearning for submission to God cooled. Maybe nobody could imagine a time apart from the electronics, the movement of events, the passions of the eras. After the plagues, the Spirit Marga reconstituted its monasteries, but the vowed members there played at their religion, at their agriculture and arts. The monasteries are places to warehouse the disenchanted and the difficult and finally, the dispossessed Children of God. From the outside, I would say they are more holding cells than places where men and women gather for a life of prayer.

Rethinking the Margas
Timothy Stillion

The actual flight back to my monastery was uneventful aside from the occasional sidelong glances the Spirit Marga troopers cast me. Soldier monks, I thought to myself. How many, scattered around the world? Leland kept his head turned to the window, a permanent frown on his scratched and bruised face. I had refused to tell him what had happened inside the destroyed building. It was not out of perverse need to have something of my own; it was simply I did not trust the people around me. I refused to give them information that would strengthen their hold on me unless I knew how that information might be used.

There was no more space to be naive.

But of course, I had only a vague idea how the Emperium would use the information that it had taken from me. No. That I had given to them.

And that did give me pause.

After the repulser-heli dropped into the fields beyond the monastery's main house, Leland turned to me. The white of one of his eyes glowed red with a burst blood vessel. "I know there's a lot you're not telling me."

"And there's a lot you're not telling me," I answered. "A lifetime of not telling me."

"We can't keep you safe without knowing everything you know."

"You can't keep me safe even if you do." I stood, ducking carefully beneath the low ceiling. I looked down at him for a moment. "Frankly, I'm not sure you even want to save me from anything."

"Your hood..." he reached into his coat, and pulled it out.

"Fuck the hood, Leland." I slipped under the hatch frame, following two soldiers ahead of me. The sun was still hours away, but fireflies sizzled among plantings. I glanced at the damage done by the helis, the tender greens smashed beneath the landing pads and illuminated with false undercarriage light. I reached up to my neckline and unfastened my habit down its right side and dropped it all into the dirt.

Leland, dipping under the hatch, paused. "What are you doing?"

"Perhaps I am leaving," I said quietly.

He froze there, as did the two soldiers.

I gestured at the nearest heli. The blades shuddered and ground to an unnatural halt. One soldier went for his side arm, but I waved two fingers at him. "Please, don't. I don't mean anyone harm."

He took aim, but Leland gestured for him to stop. "It won't work. He's already broken it. Stay where you are; he's not a killer."

"And why do you think that, Leland?"

I caught the other soldier moving out of the corner of my eye. I merely turned my gaze toward him and we all heard the harsh pop of bone breaking. He fell screaming, his hands wrapped around his knee. The other man dropped his shoulder to move on me then, but abruptly fell back, his hands clutching at his throat. I released him a moment later and he collapsed unconscious.

I looked up into Leland's eyes. "This is what you trained me for, in the forest for those month. So you tell me. Why should I stay? Ships and monks and tests and lies? Can you feel how tired I am?"

"What did that Emperium bitch do to you?"

"Blood samples, that's all. Told me a bit about my family history. Then," I said softly, smiling at him, "she offered to let me die with them."

Leland's mouth opened for just a moment, then he snapped it shut. "You don't get it, do you?" he finally sputtered. "You are going to die, only it will be out there," Leland gestured wildly to the open field. "Or worse, live a long time in a cell, poked and prodded. No skills, no home, dressed in what? A tee-shirt and pants? There will be a capture fee from the Margas and

Emperium so large on you that you'll never rest, not ever."

"Then you better not let them know I am gone." I held out my hand to him, palm up. "There are monks in play with hoods, right? Lock one of them away in my hermitage. Let everyone think I'm still there. Give me time to disappear."

"I can't do that," Leland muttered. "You know I can't do that."

I shook my head. I could feel a trembling start, there in my hands. "I'm breaking, Leland." I turned to look at the monastery hall, the soft glow from the windows. "My faith does not make it OK anymore. I bleed around the bandage of it, but God how I want to hold it all still. Spirit Marga is a story, a fiction. It is a business, a political party, and for me I fear, a prison. It has always been, and I just refused to see it." I turned back to him. "It's only a matter of time before I bring all of this down, don't you see? Let me go before I truly break, before the destruction becomes such a drug that..." I stopped, feeling my eyes growing wild within my own skull.

Leland's eyes widened, and he stepped back from me.

"It's sweet, Leland," I whispered. "Even when I fight it, it's sweet. It's powerful and addictive. I took parts of Warren from himself because it was a kind of lust. I took parts of him because I *could*. The Binder, a blooded Binder, is part of me now, and I feel it, multiplying within me. And no matter how much I submit, no matter how many times I bend my knee and say I won't use my skills, they will come out. Your ship? Do they really need someone aboard who merely breaks things? Who *lives* to break things?" I could hear my voice rising. "And the bloody awful thing, Leland? I'm not ready to die to stop myself! Because that is what it will take to finally have peace, isn't it? Offer myself up to God and throw open my arms and let you all carve me up and litter me throughout that great metal coffin that orbits us and have done with it? I can't do that," venom punctuating each word. "I won't."

"Cynta has been keeping you alive..."

"Cyntia has her own agendas." I said coldly. "And this is not life, not anymore. Once, maybe. When I could surround myself with the books and the music and plants in my garden. Before I faced the fact that I am a commodity, a boy who lived who shouldn't have, and now? A simple weapon."

Leland licked his lips. "You can have your monastic life again. You're right. I can't stop you from leaving tonight. But I'm sure Hobert and Cyntia will let you rest, replant the garden. Your skills are your bargaining chips. If you would only see the truth of it..."

"Don't," I snarled. We locked eyes, and it was Leland who looked away first.

The soldier on the ground moaned again. I shifted my gaze to him, his face in shadow, rocking against the earth. He was so young. And as quickly as it had come, the fury drained away. Like a sleepwalker, I dropped beside him, my knees sinking into the tilled soil. I was shaking hard now, but reached out and put my hands on his shattered leg. It was bad. Splinters bit through the flesh and the awful heat of the injury arced back through my own palms. I numbed the nerves, and tried not to lose myself in the quick flood of ecstasy, but it was all I could do to pull away. "He needs a medic or real Binder," I murmured. "Go. Get him help. The radio in the heli is broken."

Leland hesitated.

I looked up at him, then away. "Go! I'll keep him from bleeding to death. The other will be awake soon, too. Please, go." How tired my voice sounded.

Leland seemed to finally see the soldier I had dropped. "Promise me you'll stay with him."

"I will."

"Ianto?"

"I will!" I snapped at him. "Go!"

Leland, grinding his teeth so loudly I could hear them, whipped himself around toward the monastery and broke a run.

I kept my eyes on the young man, his face smoother now that his pain had eased, his dark hair shorn too short for his features. He was angry, in the way someone facing a shotgun is angry, a bottled outrage. I considered his clothes, musing whether or not to take them. He was about my size. People don't usually look at soldiers, I thought to myself. We don't look them in the face, and see their individuality. But in the end, I set the thought aside. He would fight me, and the pilots who waited stunned in their crafts would intervene. I had no desire to cause more pain.

"I'm sorry. I know it hurts," I murmured to him. I lifted my head, trying to gauge Leland's progress across the field, but the darkness had hidden him.

"Don't abandon us."

I turned back quickly to the young soldier. His eyes were still angry, but there was a note of broken pleading in his voice. "We've uncovered and stopped Seafarin slave sex rings, put an end to Were fighting in the New York underground. We're trying so hard to stop the pain. We're doing good things. Don't. Don't walk away from the Marga. We've heard rumors of what you can do. Now I know it's true. We need you here, on our side."

I considered him a moment, then sat down on my butt in the dirt, and drew my knees up to my chest and put my head down. "You don't understand." I felt my stomach clenching against my thighs. "I don't know what 'our side' means. The Margas are the very source of all that pain you speak of. They introduced the nanotech into the human environment and now that technology is *everywhere*, did you know that? It's why I can do what I do. They have tortured me, for lack of a better word, and twisted truth so much that I mistrust and second-guess my own instincts."

I turned my head to consider him in the twilight. "Even you, right now, I wonder who has coached you, wonder how they knew I would stay here until help returned. Almost every decision I make has been anticipated. I suspect even this one."

"Which means even if you walk away..."

"I'm still not free," I finished for him. "I know."

"Then why this show?" he asked me.

"Because I want to be a monk. A true monk," I said softly. "That's my real purpose. Not a soldier, or a dedicated healer or librarian or even a gardener. I want the thing I have been called only in name. I want to be a Child of God."

"You are," the soldier said quietly. "As are we all. That is why we have called you all this name, to remind us that you are part of us."

"But I have only felt it once, really." I glanced into the overcast darkness above us. "When I was about to die at the research facility and the glass parted for me and I fell into this life. That felt real. The rest has been a shadow dance."

"So what now?"

I looked at him, smiling bitterly. "If they are true to form, they will come with someone close to me, someone I trust or badly want to trust. And they think I will speak to them, relax, before they begin again. So, you will hear my vow now."

The soldier pressed himself up to a sitting posture. His breath caught, and I knew the nerves I had numbed were still a little at play. I could sense the breath change in the other soldier, too. I glanced his way, pitching my voice to him. "You will both hear my vow."

I stood and brushed the dirt from my pants. I picked up my robe and put it back on, and then bent for my habit hood where it had fallen from Leland's hand. Both men were sitting now, one to my right, one to my left. I stood in the dirt, the hood twisted and taut between my hands.

"We aren't priests," the young man with the broken leg murmured.

"I do this before God, and you are just my witnesses. I have no need of priests." I looked skyward, bowed to each of the four directions, touched the earth, then my heart. "I invoke the great silence. It is my vow that I will not release myself until God has shown me I may do so. I invoke the Deep Vigil. I will not release myself until God has shown me I may do so. I have been heard?"

The soldiers shifted uncomfortably. Finally the young man nodded in the half-light. "You are heard by this one."

From the other, no sound. I turned toward him, my eyes finding his. His dark skin seemed to almost melt away into the darkness. "I hurt your vocal cords, didn't I?"

He shrugged his shoulders.

"Nod and I will know I have been heard."

He nodded once, stiffly, his eyes wary.

It was enough. I pulled on my hood, feeling the odd comfort of it wrap around me. I dropped to my knees and started the long wait in silence.

Chapter 46

*Some say our Great Vigils are barbaric. I
don't agree. When a young man feels the call
to the hero's journey, he usually can't simply
sit in his cell and meditate. He needs to
physically engage that which he wants to
draw near to, be it Truth or God or simply the
knowledge of his own inner worth. The very
physicality is part of his nature. If there is an
element of brutality to the Vigils, well, it is a
nod at the warrior still present in most men.*

Understanding the Vigils
High Priestess Cyntia Molair

I didn't mark the passage of time, kneeling
like that in the soft earth. The men next to me
were respectfully quiet, although I could sense
the swelling as well as the increasing discomfort
in the young man whose leg I had snapped. His
pain sickened me, but I was afraid to do more for
him. A kind of hunger echoed in my mind, and I
would not give it rein.

I had expected a large cadre to come out of
the darkness, but in the end, only Leland, two

monks with a stretcher and Hobert appeared in a simple and open farm transport. The old abbot's hair drifted a bit around his face like a white fog, but his eyes were sharp as they scanned over the havoc I had once again caused.

He gestured impatiently for the monks to help the man with broken leg, but his eyes never left me. "Now what are you up to, Ianto?"

"He's taken the vow of silence, Abbot. And he has made known he wants the Deep Vigil." The soldier grunted with pain as his brothers shifted him onto the stretcher. "He asked us to hear him, and we did. Jacobs there, his vocal cords are damaged, but he witnessed as well."

Hobert turned to Jacobs, who nodded once, jerky. It was likely he was still very angry with me.

"I see."

I couldn't read Hobert's face. He clasped his hands behind his back, shaking his head. "Now? After your time in the woods and nearly being blown to bits, you want to undertake the Deep Vigil *now*?" He squatted before me, grimacing as his old knees complained. "And if I tell you no?"

I didn't move.

"I suppose I could have you carried back to your quarters, but then I run the risk of you breaking things, hmmm?" He shook his head then. "Maybe the Vigil is just what you need, Ianto. Many men break themselves on it. But you know that, don't you? Is that what you are hoping for?"

I held myself still, not even giving him a nod.

"You do realize that Cyntia probably would not allow this if I ask?" Hobert tried to come to his feet, and almost fell. I leaped to my feet and reached out to steady him. How gaunt he was, under his long robes. He smiled then, just a little. "We haven't made you into a machine yet, have we? From one monk to another, I give you my blessing. But I also give you the path of water, Ianto. It is the hardest of the paths, since you obviously feel you have so much to atone for." I didn't miss the irony in his voice. He turned then, heading back to the open-bedded vehicle. The monks were securing the stretcher and taking their places for the ride back to the monastery. "You will walk in," he said over his shoulder. "I will have all in readiness when you arrive at the portal."

Jacobs had come up behind my right shoulder. I stiffened, not knowing what to expect. As Hobert took his seat, he cocked his head to the side. "You wish to second his walk?"

I didn't see Jacobs nod, but Hobert shrugged. The last monk climbed into the driver's seat and Hobert gestured for him to turn around.

I waited until all I could hear were the night crickets and the steady breath of the man waiting just behind me. Perhaps it was good that we were both without a voice. I started to walk slowly, without looking at the man at my shoulder. Together, we began the long walk to the monastery.

Chapter 47

They would have made him into a submissive tool. He chose to be something quite different. There is that moment, in all of us, when we want to fling open our arms before the sword and dare life to strike us down. If cold and water was the weapon he dared to break himself upon, I should not be surprised. He was ever the child of standing, no matter how many times knocked down. He was ever the child of one more step, his own step, even into the darkness. In the end, if he opened his own veins, it was as much from curiosity to see what might catch him on the other side. How do you tame something like that?

Verbal Journal Transcripts
Sam Stelle

Hobert had gathered them all together, two long lines of monks forming a pathway between them to the northern entrance of what was simply called the Lower Temple. Jacobs broke away from my shoulder without a sound, and joined the line. I paused there, looking at the darkened stones that curved around the entrance to the below ground setting of the Deep Vigil. All around me, the classic lines of the monastery buildings reached skyward, but here, at the heart of the complex, four great pillar-framed entryways stood, with stairs leading down into the earth. The Northern Gate, the way of the cold water, was the one Hobert had assigned me. I knew that no one had completed the Great Vigil from the Northern Gate but it did not matter. I would go into the earth, and what God willed would be my own will.

I walked resolutely forward, and the assembly turned with me as I passed. Hobert waited, thin arms at his side. I drew near, and went to my knees in the dirt, hands across my chest, head bowed. He dropped a thin chain over my head. The small cylinder attached to it rested on the knuckles of my folded hands, glinting silver against my skin.

"Each shrine has a keyhole in the upper stair of each approach. When you have completed your vigil to the best of your physical ability, insert the cylinder and we will come for you."

I nodded my understanding.

"Ianto, if you can't home that key, you will be left to the water. You will die there."

Again, I nodded.

Hobert held out his hand, and I took it, coming to my feet. I was led that way, like a child, to the stone stairs leading down into the earth. He stopped then and gestured for me to go forward alone. I heard the gathered monks come to their knees. They would stay on their knees as well, this first hour, then on the first minute of each new hour of the day, they would stop their work and remind themselves that I was beneath their feet, undertaking the Vigil for them all.

I opened the first door.

The stairs were old and slick, forty to the first doorway, and narrow, room for only one. I steadied myself on the walls, my feet falling away into darkness step by step until my toe rang on the next metal door itself. It pushed away much easier than I expected. And then, another long line of stairs opened, but lit now by dim artificial lights that ran in bands down the sloping walls.

So I descended, past three more doors, long narrow stairs that had begun to curve as they dropped with me deeper into the earth. I could smell the water now, the cold dampness of the cave. And when I emerged at last into the chamber of the Deep Vigil, I drew up, stunned.

330

For a length greater than two ancient football fields, a long, narrow cavern stretched out, its oval channel of water perfectly still and reflecting the soft glow of the shrines that lined the walls. I could feel the earth above me, pressing, and marveled at the great curving walls sprung like a ribcage all down its length. I stood on a platform, with three sets of stairs, two leading down into the water, one to my left, one to my right, and one set that continued to descend into the earth directly ahead. The patterns etched into the floor curved my eye to left, and into the water there. It was where I must begin.

I undid the clasp at my throat, and drew off my hood, habit, and underclothing, folding them carefully and leaving them in the center of the platform. The chain about my neck lay cold against my skin; indeed the air itself here was chill. I knelt for the first time on the damp stones, feeling them reach out for my warmth like they were living things. I said the prayers as we had all been taught, two hours of the litany playing out in my mind. And when I was finished, I stumbled awkwardly to my feet.

Step by step, I made my way down to the water's edge. I knew it was deep, and there was no easy way to enter it except to step off. I drew in a deep breath, and plunged in.

I have never felt a cold like this, the way the body seizes all at once, everything constricting my throat, my chest. I broke the surface with a great gasp, my suddenly uncoordinated body flailing to drag itself through the frigid water. I managed to struggle my way forward, toward the first of the shrines that rimmed the cavern, and nearly cried out in relief when my hand touched the steps leading up and out of the channel.

The first shrine was elaborate, with words from the founder of Tel Na Nur, a new religion that had been birthed in the first years after the Great Reckoning. The Founder's most famous words were inscribed in the curved back wall, and the great bird that was its central image spread its tiled wings across the floor. Before the low altar, a single slab of cut quartz glowed. It was here I knelt, hands on my thighs, shivering violently.

The way of water, the Northern Gate, was a simple vigil in form. I would have to plunge into the water then enter each shrine, meditating there until I was completely dry. Then rise, sip the water, and enter it again until I could go no further. The shrine stood for each of the great world religions, moving from the present into the past. If I made it back to the beginning platform, then I could descend the stairs into the mother of shrines, where a fire burned day and night, honoring the oldest of the old.

I will not recount the passage of time in that place. Indeed, I am not sure time is a concept that would even apply. Over and over, I stepped into that terrible cold water, over and over I came to my knees on the hard quartz, drawing warmth and strength back into myself breath by breath. I suppose the Binder in me sustained my body more than any man before me, but as the hours passed, and I became weaker and more deeply chilled, my mind began to play tricks on me. I could hear voices in the water and feel the presence of others around me. I broke my vow of silence twice, crying out as if the sound had been ripped from my guts.

I had begun to feel the key at my neck, tugging for its source at each shrine. It whispered to me how easy it would be to slide it into the next hole set in the upper stair, to let them come and wrap me in warm blankets and carry me to my home. My meditation had dissolved into simple suffering, the cold so deep and intense that even thoughts lay frozen at the bottom of my mind.

I crawled up the last steps of the last shrine, unable to unbend my legs. Water ran off me, cold fingers against cold skin against cold stone. A world of cold. I looked blankly up at the Sanskrit there, the oldest of the written scriptures, and the last of these shrines to the religions of thought. The many masks of God stared down at me, their eyes blank, the water sending little ripples of light across them like momentary expressions, fleeting, distant. I curled up in a ball on the shrine floor, unable to move anymore, my own limbs folded against me offering almost no return of body heat. Use the key, my mind said sluggishly. This is as far as you can go.

As far as I could go, but not as far as I had been called. Slowly my skin dried, and I drifted into a place that felt like warmth. Such quiet here. Such peace.

But I was called onward.

Grimly, I struggled back, and slid stair by stair down into the inky, icy waters. Wooden, aching, I pulled myself along the edge of the channel to the first platform steps and shoved myself, seal-like, up their rough edges, my muscles almost useless, somewhere past even shivering. Again, I lay in the open air, drawing in on myself. Dimly, I could see the neat pile of my clothing where I had left them, miles away to my one open eye.

"Get up," my mind whispered somewhere in a dark corner. "Get up. There is fire below, down into the cave of the God without voice, the God before thought, the I AM, the resounding That."

And somehow I did, inch by inch, half-crawling to the downward stairs. I slid my legs around, and pushed myself down the first steps then leaned against the cold stone wall, shuddering, levering myself up its face, clinging to it with numb fingers. I stepped down cautiously, step by step, moving sideways, both hands pressed now to the wall for support.

I'm not sure what happened then, a foot slipping, a leg giving way, but I lost my balance and fell, sliding a few feet on my left hip, then chest. I scraped at the wall, clawing to stop my descent. I lay there gasping, shaking, and resting my head on the stones.

"Get up," my mind said again.

I didn't, though. I eased myself down to the next step, then the next, my body close to the stairs, my eyes closed, feeling what I could with my body. I was bleeding badly from my hip and chest, and knew I was leaving a long trail of blood down the steps.

When I finally reached the lower door, I curled up against the heavily embossed metal, breathing heavily. For some time I rested there, wanting only to feel the firm support of the door, the little warmth my descent had brought to my aching body. Then, I was clawing my way up again, and the door opened before my gentle shove.

Beyond, a small cave waited for me. A fire burned in the middle, and the ceiling curved overhead, so close I could barely stand. I stumbled toward it, weaving, one hand sealed to my hip. Even my blood felt cold, seeping through the fingers of my hand and the breath burned in my chest.

I collapsed near the fire and though it was forbidden in the vigil, I had no choice but to let the darkness finally take me.

Chapter 48

The demands of operating under the wings of a good defense have always been reliant on trusting who or what is defending you. Otherwise, you have created a nearer enemy, a deadlier enemy.

Level One Text
Armed Services of the Emperium

I opened my eyes to the fire. My hands were sticky with blood, my chest and hip aching. For a while all I could do was watch the flames.

Finally, I pushed myself up, my head thrown back and mouth open in pain. I rolled to my knees, shuddering. My head fell then and hung between my braced arms as I willed myself to complete the vigil.

It was some time before I was able to raise my head a little. The gentle curve of the cave wobbled with the firelight. There were no words of wisdom here, no sculptures, no paintings, only living rock. Around the fire pit, four shallow bowls stood watch, each with a slim knife lying flat between it and the fire. Beyond them, a larger black bowl nestled against the base of the wall. The deep silence of the earth above and around me pervaded the place, and called to an old part of my blood.

There had been no training about this place, no rituals passed down, no music, nothing to hold onto except the still pregnant earthiness of the presence, the God of no name, no image. So when I heard the sigh of Her voice, I could feel the sudden pounding of my heart in my chest.

"I am becoming not myself," the voice said. It echoed around the cave, seeping from the rocks themselves like a breath, but also punctuated by the snapping dance of the fire. "He must be broken. Your hands now, from my heart." Three times she said it, clear and distinct. I reached out with all my senses, but could find no hint of sophisticated technology here in the bowels of the earth. And when her voice faded away again, my ears ached with the silence.

He must be broken.

We're all broken already, I thought to myself. God, my unconscious, a technology I could not hear, what did it matter? Always the same, I was called to break things.

He must be broken.

Here, at the end of the vigil there were no answers. Here, at the place from which all ideas of God sprang, only the same message.

He must be broken.

Did God want broken things? Very well, then She could take me. I pulled the silver chain over my head and tossed it in the very center of the fire. I watched it for a time, the way the links folded over and around the logs like a vine. Then I reached down for one of the little daggers that lay on the earth by the bowl at my knees. Eyes still on the fire, I slashed across my wrist. I cut deep.

In a haze, I crawled around the fire, flowing my blood into each bowel like a dark shadow, then crept toward the last vessel, hunkering against the wall. The Binder in me was screaming, trying to heal the rapid flow of blood, but the killer in me held it back. Not this time, not this time, I chanted in my mind.

He must be broken.

I couldn't make it to the last bowl. I felt myself hit the ground, my face scraping on stone. I felt my hand creep out and start writing with my finger across the floor, something I didn't understand, a kind of vow? My last words?

And then he was there, stretched out beside me, his face so close but still so indistinct to my eye. "What the hell are you doing?" My elf reached out and I could feel his fingers brush back my damp hair. He seemed so real, so solid. But I didn't answer him, only looked through him and smiled brokenly.

I was vowed to silence.

It felt as if he had gently gathered me up, his fingers knitting around my slashed wrist, putting pressure there. I leaned my head against his chest, against his heartbeat and breath. He rocked me a little, his lips close to my ear. "Gods, what a mess you've made of yourself. We are a pair, aren't we? But I'm not ready to let you go. Not ready. Not ready. And neither are you." He raised his head. "Please. Call them down, reach out and call them down here. Do it now."

I pointed weakly to the fire where the key was melting against the wood.

He bent over my ear again. "I wasn't talking to you. Stay still. Stay here with me."

I shut my eyes, lulled by his voice and rocking. I could hear him continuing to talk to me, but the words weren't making sense anymore. I felt light, spacious.

Time passed, as time does.

And when my eyes opened again, I knew at once it was not my elfin friend anymore who held me, but the towering Binder Tebre.

Chapter 49

The years after the Great Reckoning were quite rich in some ways. We experienced an anguished and raw outpouring of music, theater, artwork, writing. That's what we humans do, though. Redeem suffering, transform it, make it art. Then go on. Always, pick up and go on.

Humanities and the Great Reckoning
Suzanna Sloan

Tebre lifted me effortlessly, carrying me up the steep and slippery rock stairs to the platform, then over the terrible flight of steps to the surface. At the end, I could feel her labored breath, hear the grunts as she took those last steps before she laid me on the ground beneath the sun.

Others were there, it seemed, covering me. I could feel Tebre reaching in, stabilizing me. I shook my head, pushed at her, but she tenderly ignored it, batting my hands away. "Stop it," she murmured. "Ianto, stop it. I heard you. I came.

You don't want to die. I know you too well. Now let me work; you've made a mess of yourself."

How had she heard me? I thought weakly. I, under a vow of silence so strict that I would not even speak to my elf when I had the last chance to do so. I closed my eyes and let her do as she wished.

Then I was lifted again. I could feel the jounce of a transport and finally my body being covered familiar sheets and blankets. I could hear wondering whispers, felt hands reach out to touch me as if I were a talisman. I shrank from them all, and finally sensed that Tebre had driven them from my hermitage. And then she was resting her hands on me. I could feel the familiar thrum of her healing work lulling me to sleep.

I woke the next day to her gentle snores. She had pulled a chair over by my bed, and now was curved over herself, asleep. I reached out slowly, painfully, and touched her leg. She startled awake, blinking rapidly, then her eyes found my face and she smiled tiredly. "You're so incredibly stupid, do you know that?" she murmured.

I nodded. Even that little movement hurt.

"Hobert tells me you are under a vow of silence."

I nodded again. I could feel my eyes resting on her face, feel them shining with tears I was loathe to shed. I touched my heart with three fingers, holding them up, then touched her own.

"I know. I can't believe Warren is gone, either," she murmured. "But I am glad the two of you made peace. Or at least that is what they told me."

I smiled sadly. We sat there for a time, as if saying goodbye to Warren all over again.

How did you do it?" she finally asked in a quiet voice. "How did you reach into my head and tell me to come?"

I touched my lips and heart and shook my head.

"But I know it was you. It felt just like you," Tebre said. "It's really annoying not being able to talk about it, Ianto."

I chuckled, and reached out for her hand. She held it silently for a time.

"Why did you write that message in your own blood?" she finally asked me.

I shook my head, not understanding.

"You wrote that 'when Cyntia calls, I will go.'"

I frowned and shook my head again. I felt myself swallow as I tried to remember what I had written. I dimly recalled my fingers moving over the stone, but that was all I could bring to mind.

Tebre sighed, and brushed a lock of dark hair off my forehead. "You weren't yourself. I'm not surprised there's a lot you don't remember, Ianto."

I am becoming not myself. He must be broken. The words flooded back into my mind. Tebre must have seen the recognition dawn across my face because she leaned forward, alarmed. "Ianto?"

I pulled my hand away, and tried to sit up. My side ached and the room spun crazily for a moment. Tebre came to her feet, and put a hand on each shoulder, physically holding me to the bed. She wasn't rough, but she was uncompromising. "Stop it," she said. "You had three broken ribs, you're bruised just about everywhere else, and you tried to cut your own damn hand off...do you want me to continue the litany? Lie down."

I did, almost gratefully.

"Hobert will come in the morning. Until then, I will sit with you, and you will rest, do you understand?"

I closed my eyes, too tired to even grind my teeth at the edges of frustration. She laid her hand on my shoulder gently. "You'll tell me all about it one day. Rest now. I didn't mean to disturb you so earlier. I'll keep the silence with you." I could feel the Binder's touch calming my muscles, reaching within me softly. And after a time, I slept.

Chapter 50

We will need a new faith to explain and ease the changes of our times. Or perhaps only a very old one that sees this all—nanotech, children of God, Margas and Emperium, plagues and art--as layla, the play of God. Or perhaps we have only to see all of this as Maya, while the Unborn One looks out at us from our own mirrors and winks.

Drunken Days
High Priestess Cyntia Molair

Tebre left nearly four days later. I could tell she was disappointed that I could not or would not speak with her, but she kissed me on my forehead and told me that she would always be there for me. I watched her walk up my cloistered garden path from my doorway then turned back to my small cabin. I stood there, just inside, feeling the walls so close. In the end, I simply slid down the doorframe and sat there.

By evening, I roused myself enough to eat a bit. The golden light was slanting across the garden, and illuminating a small cloud of gnats dancing over the plants. I dropped my eyes to my table, to the hood that lay neat and waiting for me. After I had cleaned up my plate, I put it on. The familiar mesh closed around my sight, muffled my hearing. It was, in its own way, like snuggling into a well-loved blanket. I sat and put my head back down on the table and fell asleep.

The knock at my door startled me and for a moment I sat there, blinking in confusion and even a bit of fear. It took me a while to unwind myself enough to answer the door.

Hobert stood on the stoop, his head cocked a bit and eyes narrow. A breezed ruffled what was left of his white hair. "You've put the hood back on."

I nodded at the obvious. I couldn't tell, though, if he were pleased or concerned.

"Come out here, Ianto. I have something to tell you, something you will need to consider very carefully."

I touched my lips through the mesh.

"I know," Hobert said. "I'll talk. You listen. Is that OK?"

I nodded and followed him out into the garden, to the little bench where Jean and I had sat and talked. Had it been such a short time ago? I stood until the old man had seated himself, straight-backed and hands on his knees. He looked up at me expectantly and patted the hard cement. "Sit down, Ianto."

I sat. The garden buzzed around us, magical with morning light.

"Cyntia has asked that I bring you an assignment."

For a moment, Tebre's voice echoed in my head, how I had written in blood that I would go where Cyntia asked. I swallowed hard, my jaw knit.

"The Science Marga would like a house priest assigned to them."

I immediately shook my head, touching my chest.

Hobert grasped my wrist and forced my hand down to my own lap. I pulled it away, a little roughly. "I know you are not a priest, but the duties there are not ritualistic, but rather intellectual in nature. Listen to me. Science Marga is seeking to better understand a Game that they created, and in doing so, better understand what has happened and what may happen to the Children of God. Originally the game program and its attendant AI, Nuress, were meant to support the mind of a young man named Sam Stelle, son of Edwere Stelle, the head of the Science Marga. Sam had an unfortunate accident over ten years ago that caged his mind in an unresponsive body. Edwere only wanted to give his child some semblance of life. But it has grown to be something much more than was originally intended. Cyntia believes you can help them study what is evolving within the game. And so do I."

He placed a hand on my knee, and I jerked in spite of myself.

He immediately withdrew his touch, shaking his head in apology. "I know you are still raw, Ianto. Nobody has gone so far in the Deep Vigil. You're a hero to the monks here."

He shifted on the stone. "And I know what you suffered in the forest trials. I know you are probably not ready for more change. All I ask is that we sit together here, and so that you might consider how to be of purpose, how you might now *serve*. And if you decide to go, will you do one thing for me?"

I sat waiting in silence.

"Would you write down the story of your life so far? For the archives?"

None of his words were particularly appealing. So I sat there with him in silence, holding pools of sunlight in my green robes, and trying to be nothing more than a plant dug deep in the soil. In the end, I knew I would go, just as I knew I would write it all down for him.

No, not for him. Because High Priestess Cyntia of the Spirit Marga had asked, because something *knew* Cyntia would ask, and it was for that mystery I would go to the Mansion of the Science Marga.

The story of Ianto and Samu'el continues in:
Children of the Great Reckoning
Firewall:
Book II: Samu'el
by
K.B. Nelson

Character List

Hobert Temmons: Abbot of the Northwest Monastery, advisor to Cyntia Molair.

Ianto Tobali: A genetically-modified and nanotech-infected Child of God who has the unique ability to reach out to his environment and "break" living and non-living matter as well as bind it to him. Spirit Marga wants to refine its control over him in order to use his special talents.

Jean Molair: Priestess of the Spirit Marga, daughter of High Priestess of the Spirit Marga, Cyntia Molair.

Cyntia Molair: High Priestess of the Spirit Marga, one of the three great socio-political entities to survive the plagues that ravaged Earth.

Sam (Samu'el) Stelle: son of Edwere Stelle, critically injured as a child and sent into the Game. He dreams the elements of the Game and the central AI, Nuress, crafts his thoughts into a continuous alternate reality. His is the only real mind within the entire world of the Game. He most often manifests as a blond elf and is later bonded to Ianto by Nuress, the Game's AI.

Leland: Soldier-Monk of the Spirit Marga and attaché to Cyntia Molair.

Elrica: A blooded Binder in the Game—a huge species of humanoid, nearly seven feet tall with black hair and red eyes. Binders are healers, but can be twisted to become something very much like vampires.

Tebre: A Binder in reality, a gentle healer who lives in the forest of the Pacific Northwest.

Warren: Blooded Binder and also a healer monk of the Spirit Marga.

Vic: Human hunter of the Children of God

Petrek: Senior Nanite Tech for the Emperium. A previous employee of the Science Marga and one of the creators of the Game which houses Sam Stelle's consciousness.

Nuress: The child-avatar for the guiding artificial intelligence of the Game.

Edwere Stelle: Executive Head of the Science Marga, father of Sam and Larisa Stelle. Creator of the Game, a virtual reality world that interfaces directly with the nervous systems of the players via their nanotech.

About the Author

K.B. Nelson holds a master's degree in comparative religion and loves teaching yoga, qigong and adult education classes when she is not writing, crafting fiber art or running after the sheep in her backyard. "My grandfather once said he was a jack of all trades and master of none. I think I have managed to live into that same sentiment my whole life, and I can't say it has ever disappointed me." Kim has authored three non-fiction titles and five science fiction works and her poetry has appeared in both national anthologies and national magazines.

www.ingramcontent.com/pod-product-compliance
Lightning Source LLC
Chambersburg PA
CBHW062009170626
46813CB00001B/86